PERFECT SEAS

A Grey's Harbor Story

JENNIFER SIVEC

Edited by
JC WING

Illustrated by
KATE CONWAY

SOUL SISTER PRESS

For Robin and JC because without them there would be no paradise like Grey's Harbor.

C hloe

"Go to your room and change, immediately." Chloe looked down at the small figure in front of her wearing the pink tutu, red and white striped t-shirt with a purple marker stain, red leggings, and bright yellow rain boots.

The large blue eyes on the tiny face that so resembled her own begged her not to be mad but Chloe was immune. She'd learned that if she softened too much, she'd regret it later.

"But Momm-eeeee. You said to get dressed and this is what I wanted to wear." The lip came out before she could stop herself and she tucked it back in as fast as she could.

Chloe's hand quickly came within inches of Savi's face and stopped when she saw that she had put her lip back where it belonged.

"Did you even look in the mirror?" Chloe huffed. "You look like a homeless child, and I'm not going to be seen in public with someone dressed like you."

Savi blinked hard like she'd been slapped.

For a moment, Chloe wanted to take back the harshness of her words. After all, Savi was only seven, and she couldn't help that she didn't know how to match her clothes. She looked down at her daughter and fought the urge to take her in her arms.

She didn't want to spoil her.

Kids needed discipline and if she hugged her, she would send the wrong message. Her mother had been hard on her and it had served her well. She had swiftly risen through the ranks of her company and was the youngest female executive.

If she could run a company, she could certainly make sure her child was dressed appropriately for a visit with her grandparents.

"Go. Change!" Chloe pointed up the stairs and immediately Savi did a turnaround and ran as fast as her little legs would take her.

Chloe sat down at the kitchen table and rubbed her temple as she tried to sip her coffee and ignore her grumbling stomach. She hadn't eaten before noon in years and she wasn't going to start now, no matter how hungry she was.

Coffee.

All I need is coffee.

Damn! Still too hot!

She tried to ignore the pulsing that told her that a headache would be coming soon. She'd been getting a lot of headaches lately, which she attributed to stress. Getting promoted hadn't been easy, but she had busted her ass to do it, winning out over four other candidates.

She'd been working more than ever, but she'd promised her parents a visit. It was only one day she'd have to see them, and it had been a while, but of course Brent had a work trip already planned that he couldn't change.

"I'm sorry." He was apologetic as always. Their time together had diminished over the past year to hurried chaste kisses hello and good-bye, and as much as they'd tried to schedule time together, it hadn't happened in what felt like forever.

Then a few months before she found the picture on his phone of the naked bald vagina that wasn't hers. He had sworn on Savi's life that it was a screenshot of one he found on the internet but then he finally confessed that it belonged to someone he'd met. She meant nothing to him, he'd insisted, but she could see in his eyes that he was lying and knew she would never be able to trust him again.

"I don't understand why you need to go on this trip." Chloe was annoyed. "You were just gone for an entire week last month and I need more notice than that so that I can make arrangements for Savi."

"I'm sorry but I have to, Chlo." He'd looked uncomfortable. "Joe got the flu and they asked me fill in. They might want me to start hitting the road more, which is good for my career."

She knew that his work was as demanding as hers and she could hardly blame him, but he'd always been her rock. Her safe place. She was still trying to get used to the idea that he wasn't any longer. She was convinced his affair with the slut he was sleeping with would pass eventually and thought she might want to take him back, but she wasn't sure. She didn't know if she loved him that much.

He'd left the night before and would be gone for a week, and Savi would be spending a lot of time with the nanny.

Chloe hated that but it couldn't be helped.

She looked down at her watch.

"Savi," she called up the stairs. "Hurry up. Nonny and Poppy are waiting!"

She fought the frustration that she couldn't seem to push away these days and cursed under her breath. Her mother had warned her that being a parent was hard.

"Maybe you're not cut out to be a mother, Chlo. Motherhood requires warmth and patience, and you have neither of those things. You have no idea the strain that being your mother has put on me. It's not for the faint of heart. I just don't know if you'd ever be capable." Chloe could repeat the familiar speech in her sleep. She'd heard it at five, then ten, then sixteen, then twenty. At twenty-four she thought she might try, but now she didn't feel at all like she was getting it right.

She hated that her mother didn't believe in her at all. Then again, the only daughter her mother had shown any faith in life was Abi, and now her granddaughter, Savi.

Abi had been the favorite.

Abi could do no wrong.

But now Abi lived five hours away and refused to come home to

Grey's Harbor to visit, even for a weekend. Chloe felt guilty that she resented her sister, but Chloe had lived in a cold world her entire life, while Abi had soaked up the warmth of her mother's love. Chloe never understood it.

She was the oldest and had done everything right, but she could see in her parents' eyes how much they adored Abi, so Chloe had given up trying to please them early on, fighting against them every chance she got just to prove them wrong. She tried to tell herself that she didn't need their approval, but deep down she knew she was wrong.

Savi finally bounded down the stairs, no remnants of her former outfit remaining. She wore a plain pink cotton dress with polka dots and little white socks with frilly lace on the cuff. Her pink tennis shoes were tied perfectly.

"Much better!" Chloe exclaimed. "Nonny will like that outfit so much better!"

Chloe kissed Savi on top of her head, taking in the smell of baby shampoo. She regretted getting so angry with her, but Savi needed to learn how to listen.

She often forgot that she was just a little girl and tried to remember being Savi's age but couldn't. It was as though the memories had been erased and replaced with a fuzzy collection of pictures from her childhood and stories that seemed familiar but not quite real.

"You had a wonderful childhood, Chloe," her mom had assured her. "Why would you ever think differently?"

Chloe rubbed her temple again and tried to chase the impending headache away.

"Please get your coat, Savi. We have to meet Nonny at ten and she doesn't like it when we're late." Chloe took another sip of her coffee and closed her eyes.

If she could just get through the morning, the rest of the day would be smooth sailing.

It'll be fine, she reassured herself.

What could possibly go wrong?

eena

THE LIGHT ON HER PHONE GLOWED BRIGHT IN THE DARK BEDROOM.
Neena groaned. She had just fallen asleep.

I need to see you.

She read the text, her brain half asleep. She didn't recognize the
number.

Please, doll.

Neena sighed. The familiar nickname was one she hadn't seen in
months.

She laid the phone facedown on the nightstand and tried to go
back to sleep but she knew it was useless because she would never
sleep now.

She tried to think back to the last time she'd been called *doll*.

She had been through this time and again and it never ended well,
but something deep inside made her want to respond more than
anything.

She fought the urge to pick up the phone even though she knew she shouldn't. It was like an addiction, this relationship, and she hated to admit how much she wanted it.

How much she needed it.

Just ignore it, she told herself. If I ignore it, it might go away. But even as she told herself that she knew better she wanted nothing more than to text back. It was the same pattern, and no matter what she did, or how many times she told herself that it would be different, it never was.

Her thoughts immediately went to her dad.

She knew what he would say. He'd been saying it her entire life, yet she'd refused to listen, always believing it would be different this time.

"Neena, you deserve so much better. Stop feeding into the craziness! You have to let this go, sweetheart."

Daddy was right. He was right about everything, and of all people, he always knew best. He'd known heartache better than anyone, yet he still wasn't bitter. He was the same sweet guy he'd always been.

"How do I let it go, Daddy?" She'd tried and never could.

"You just have to close your heart to the wrong people and open it to the right ones."

It had sounded so simple, but Neena couldn't figure out how to do it. It seemed as though her heart had only been created to be broken.

Her phone lit up again.

Please, doll. I'm sorry about the last time. I don't know why I did what I did. Please. Don't ignore me.

Neena knew that if she answered it, the end result might break her for good this time.

Chaos.

Destruction.

Heartache.

She knew she couldn't keep doing this to herself, or sweet Jaden. There was more than just her to think about now. She had to protect her baby brother. It was her job to make sure his childhood was better than hers had been. She just wasn't sure she had the strength to make it happen.

Her fingers crept toward the phone and she picked it up and reread the message.

I need to see you. I'm so sorry about the last time. I would never hurt you intentionally. I don't know why I always hurt you because I do love you.

Neena slowly reread every word.

I do love you.

She'd waited to hear those words her entire life and there they were on her phone.

She typed fast and hit send before she could stop herself. She stared at the screen for what felt like forever as she waited for a response but there was none.

She glanced at the clock. 2:30 AM. She groaned as she sank back against the pillows.

She knew she would never get any sleep now.

Just then the door opened slowly.

"Nee," a small voice whispered in the dark.

"Jaden, what are you doing up?" Neena sat up. She heard the tiny patter of soft pajama'd feet on the wood floor, and as they got closer, she bent over and swept his tiny body up on the bed.

"I not sleepy." He shoved his thumb in his mouth and started sucking, a sign to Neena that he was indeed tired.

"Do you want to lay here with me for a little while?" Neena asked kissing his forehead. She closed her eyes and breathed him in.

"Yes!" he said, his response muffled by his thumb.

Neena snuggled him in close and rested her chin on the top of his head. At five years old, he was the love of her life. She had never imagined that she could ever love anyone as much, but she knew from the moment she saw him that she could never love anyone more.

"I wuv you, Nee." Jaden's tired voice was barely above a whisper.

She listened for the sound of his steady breathing so she would know he was finally asleep. She closed her eyes and begged sleep to come, but her mind continued to race.

It had been months since she had gotten a text like that one and she hated herself for getting so excited.

She had told herself after the last time she would never put herself in that situation ever again. She had not only been emotionally hurt but nearly physically as well. She knew that the danger was escalating but she couldn't stay away.

She knew she deserved better, but she was like an addict. She needed the love that was always promised, but never delivered, on the other side of the text. She yearned for it and she needed it more than anything else in her life.

Daddy had taught her that love was complicated. He had told her that it could hurt like hell, and she believed him because she'd seen it for herself. She'd felt the ache and the emptiness of wanting what she couldn't have.

I need to see you.

She needed it, too.

She knew she'd have to tell Daddy, but she would deal with that when it was time.

Maybe this time would be different? Maybe things had changed. People changed all the time, didn't they? She'd always believed that people could.

Maybe this time it would be different.

3

G ina

GINA WALKED THROUGH THE IMMACULATE LIVING ROOM, HER EYES darting from corner to corner to make sure nothing was out of place. She went room to room, inspecting the house as she always did after she had done a thorough cleaning.

It was her favorite thing to do because in that brief moment, everything was perfect, which meant that she was, too.

She knew it would only last for a moment.

She knew the moment the children walked in that they would wreck the place and she sighed. No matter how many times she told Lincoln to hang his backpack up, he always left it on the floor right inside the door. Leo was no better. He followed his brother everywhere he went and did everything he did.

They were the spitting image of one another, and both favored Theo with their dark hair and dark eyes. They were sweet and loving, but little boys were like tornados. Small and adorable tornados.

She had always made Theo promise that if they ever had a son, they had to name him after her brother and Theo had kept his promise. When Lincoln was born, she was instantly in love. Her sons made her heart melt and she loved them so deeply, in a way she imagined her parents had never loved her or Linc.

She had grown up worrying that she wouldn't know how to be a mother but when the boys were born, they instantly wrapped around her heart and made it impossible for her to feel anything less than true love.

The thought of harming them in any way seemed completely alien to her no matter how careless or dirty they were.

No matter how much she adored them they were messy little monsters, and she always ended up picking up after them because they were seven and six and she indulged their youth.

She shuddered as she remembered how her parents had refused to allow her and her brother to leave even one thing out of place in their bedrooms. They hadn't cared about their feelings, but they expected them to keep the house spotless. Gina always thought it was a strange requirement considering how little they cared about anything else.

If they didn't, there had been consequences, and they had been ugly.

She thought back to when she had forgotten to put the dishes away when she was seven. Her mother had been so angry with her and she had been forced to kneel in the closet for the entire evening without dinner.

It was the last time she had forgotten about the dishes, but there were other offenses that she had paid dearly for.

Linc had it worse than her. He was the oldest and took the brunt of it. At eighteen, he ran away, and she hadn't seen him since. He had been her only shelter, and she felt his absence like there was an enormous hole right in center of her being every day.

Even after she'd graduated high school and gone away to college, she still looked for him and hoped he'd know where she was. It had been fifteen years and he was still nowhere to be found.

Gina swiped at a tear that slipped out of the corner of her eye. She was angry at him for abandoning her and leaving her there with them, but mostly she just missed him.

She bent over under little Lincoln's bed and pulled out a pair of dirty underwear. She was always pulling dirty clothes out from under his bed and she wondered what would ever make him discard them there?

She never understood boys.

After she double-checked the rooms one last time, she finally allowed herself to have a cup of tea.

No sugar, no cream.

Black only. She couldn't afford the extra calories.

She closed her eyes and took a long, deep breath. Wednesdays were her least favorite day. It was house-cleaning day and it was exhausting. She cleaned every day, but Wednesdays were the day she scoured from top to bottom.

Theo had asked her to hire someone to help but she refused. Taking care of the house was the only job she had and she couldn't leave it up to someone else. She would feel too guilty allowing someone else to do her job.

She had always told herself it was the price she paid for living in her dream home and never having to work again. She told herself that this was her job. To keep the house clean, do laundry, and take care of the kids. Lord knew that her husband, Theo, did enough.

She didn't mind and was proud of her immaculate home. She had always thrown herself into anything she was committed to with everything she had.

This just wasn't what she had imagined for her life.

Her favorite days were gym days. Those were the days she'd spend hours at the gym, working out all of the darkness that lay just below the surface and permeated through her. She'd move from the treadmill, to the elliptical, to the stair climber. She might even take in a spin class or yoga. The sweat would pour off of her and she would imagine it was the poison that lived inside, threatening to consume her. She pushed hard to make sure there was nothing left, and she'd leave the gym after several hours feeling empty, until the next time.

When she was younger, she ran. For miles and miles, she ran as hard and fast as she could. Running away from and running toward a life that was very different from the one she had been raised in.

She needed her gym days. Without them, she wasn't sure she would make it through the week. Today wasn't a gym day though. It was Wednesday, and she knew she'd need to get through today just to get to tomorrow so she could go to the gym.

She was anxious about the party that was coming up and the house needed to be perfect. Theo had offered to pay a service, but he was already spending a fortune on the catering and a band, and she persuaded him to let her take care of the house.

She wished that she hadn't been such a martyr. There was a lot to clean and it had taken her longer than usual. At least she had agreed to let him bring someone in the day of the party just to tidy things up one last time.

"You don't have time for that, Ginny." He intentionally kissed her on the neck, her greatest weakness, and she had relented.

She sipped her tea and thought what she would do if she only had five minutes to herself. She envisioned the canvases that sat in a corner of the attic, unwrapped and untouched. She pictured her paintbrushes that she had painstakingly cleaned years ago and stored safely but hadn't picked up for entirely too long. She had been an art major in college when she and Theo met, but had dropped out when she'd gotten pregnant.

Theo told her she should paint again, but she had refused. There weren't enough hours in the day, she had told him. The truth was, she knew what would happen if she began painting again. She would lose herself in it and neglect the house and her family.

She had been obsessive about her art, and now the life she had worked so hard to cultivate for herself and her family was her only purpose.

"Maybe when the kids are older and I have more free time," she told Theo who seemed satisfied with the answer.

She took another sip of her tea and glanced at the clock. It was nearly time for the kids to get off the bus. She took another big gulp and carefully washed out the mug and put it away. It occurred to her that she hadn't eaten anything all day as she ignored the grumbling in her stomach.

There was no time as she mentally prepared herself to handle the children. She took one last look around the sparkling kitchen with satisfaction and a small smile.

The monsters would be home in two minutes.

And she waited.

4

A bi

THE FIGHTING COMING FROM THE KID'S ROOM WOKE ABI FROM A
sound sleep.

She glanced at the clock and groaned. She had only been asleep for
three hours, working the late shift. It had been a crazy one the night
before, but she had raked in the tips and it had been worth it.

Her alarm was set to go off in five minutes.

She pulled herself up, her body straining. She rubbed her sore back
and reminded herself that she was only twenty-five years old. Her door
flew open and both kids came barreling in.

Dominic turned on the light, temporarily blinding her. "Mommy!"
Lexi screamed. "Tell him to stop"

"Sissy won't share her iPad!" He pointed at his sister, angrily

"But its mine!" Lexi burst into tears.

Abi took a deep breath. "I told you when Mommy works late you
have to stay in bed until I come and get you! Mommy is exhausted!"

She tried to ignore the bickering, but they refused to stop, both kids crying.

"I don't give a damn about your iPad. I'll break it and then neither one of you will be able to play with it!" she raged, regretting it instantly.

Both children stared, their big blue eyes fixed on her, and she immediately felt horrible.

She reminded herself that she did not want to turn into her father, but her words echoed in a distant memory from childhood. Even though she knew Chloe had been yelled at the most when they were kids, she'd still heard it. Abi had been the baby and they treated her like one, always catering to her needs while they reprimanded Chloe even when she'd breathed in the wrong direction.

It had caused a rift between them throughout their adult life, even though Chloe denied it. Chloe had moved out as soon as she'd turned eighteen, but Abi had been twelve. She hated to admit that she resented Chloe for leaving.

Abi knew without anyone saying that Chloe was the favorite now. Chloe was the perfect mom and the big executive, and Abi was the fuck up who couldn't go home because her husband had left her after she'd fought so hard to be with him.

She gathered both kids into her arms. "I'm sorry. Mommy is just very tired. I worked until three o'clock in the morning. While you were sleeping, I was working so that you can have toys and things like your iPad."

Both kids nodded. At seven and eight they were incredibly intuitive, and Abi reminded herself often how lucky she was. But being the lone parent was exhausting, and she fought being overpowered by the weight of it every day.

"Please go back to bed." Abi tried to keep the desperation out of her voice, but she would've killed for another half hour of sleep.

She kissed them on the head and they went back to their rooms without another sound.

As she sank back into the bed, she pulled the soft blankets over herself and tried to disappear. It had been a hard few years. Her ex had left her for someone they'd gone to high school with, and even though she knew she should go back home to Grey's Harbor, she just couldn't.

He had blindsided her when he left, and she was humiliated because she thought they were happy and in love. At least she had been.

She had never doubted him, and when they got pregnant in high school, she wasn't worried even though they were so young. He already had a job lined up away from home and she had no choice but to go with him.

She'd picked up her entire life, seven months pregnant, and as soon as she graduated from high school, she followed him.

She hadn't known it at the time, but it had been the biggest mistake of her life.

He had been too much of a wuss to own up to what he'd done, having an affair through Facebook and then meeting her when he was supposed to be on work assignments. Instead, she had to find out when his new girlfriend texted her and told her she was pregnant.

It turned out it was the girlfriend he'd dated before her.

I'm having your man's baby. That's karma, bitch!

Cat had always been convinced that Abi had stolen him from her even though she hadn't. But it didn't matter now. He was leaving her and there was nothing left to say.

He had already moved back home but she was too ashamed. Chloe had made something of herself and her parents thought she was the better sister. She'd married well, had a high-paying job, a handsome husband, and the perfect child. Not to mention the big house on the north side of Grey's Harbor.

Abi was jealous but more than that, she was embarrassed. Five hours was a long way to be from home without family, but she knew what her mom would say.

"I told you that he was a deadbeat the moment you brought him home, Abigail! If you'd ever listen to someone once in a while."

Abi had told her mom on the phone and could almost see her face. She'd have that scowl that she always got when she was angry, the lines furrowed deep between her eyes.

The only thing Abi had inherited from her was her blue eyes. She looked more like Chloe than her own mother, and she was thankful. Chloe was the taller version of the two and kept her hair fashionably short and meticulous, while Abi's always flowed wild, their hair reflecting their personalities.

Abi wanted nothing more than to go back to school and finish her nursing degree which was what she had been doing when her Todd left, but at twenty-five she felt like she was eighty. The flexibility of her job allowed her to work double shifts, but she missed seeing the kids and she needed so much more for them.

She closed her eyes and tried to convince herself to sleep for just a little while, but sleep was elusive, and her brain begin to tick away at the bills that were coming up.

She already knew that she would need to pick up an extra shift or two for the holidays. She wanted to get both kids their one big special gift. She knew she could ask her parents, and her mom had been begging her to come home this year. She hadn't decided if she wanted to return to the small town where she found and lost the love of her life, and she didn't want to run into him.

It was likely she would, and she wasn't sure if she or the kids could stand it. He hadn't even called them since he'd left, and they were beginning to ask for him less and less.

She listened for the kids, but they had gone back to their rooms and were quiet. She whispered a prayer of thanks and closed her eyes.

"Come and visit, Abigail. It's been too long since you've been home." Mom hadn't made it sound like she was giving her an option.

She wasn't sure what to do but as she continued to mentally calculate the bills that were due, she knew she was running out of time.

C hloe

CHLOE AND SAVI RUSHED INTO THE LIBRARY AT FIVE MINUTES AFTER ten, and Children's Reading Time was already in full swing. Savi was thrilled to see Miss Magnolia Jane, the children's librarian, and the biggest reason she loved visiting the library.

"You'll have to forgive Chloe," Anita Caldwell said loudly. "If this was a meeting with my daughter's executive board, she would be ten minutes early."

Magnolia Jane smiled graciously and waved Savi over to sit next to her.

"Hello, Mom." Chloe leaned over and kissed Anita on the cheek. She ignored the jab at her tardiness. She'd been hearing it her entire life and she always expected it.

Savi gave Nonny a quick kiss, and then ran off to listen to stories with the other children.

Chloe sat across from Anita and watched Savi who earnestly seemed to enjoy the story.

"You look good. Did you lose a couple of pounds? Your face looks thinner than usual."

"Maybe, I don't pay attention to that, Mom." Chloe tried to hide her irritation. As a teenager, her weight was the topic of numerous conversations. As an adult, Chloe maintained a size two, and no longer had patience with her mother on the topic.

"Okay, well you don't have to bite my head off," Anita huffed.

"I'm sorry, Mom. I'm just tired and I have a terrible headache." Chloe had been fighting it all morning but realized she no longer had a choice but to succumb to the pounding in her head.

She knew it was the price she paid for her high-stress position at the firm and her hectic life, but she was getting them more often and they were becoming a disruption. She fumbled in her purse for her pain medication.

"That's still no reason to take it out on me." Anita pouted.

Chloe knew she'd done it now. There would be no pacifying her, and she'd have to hear about her crimes all morning.

"You're right. I'm sorry." Chloe looked around desperately for a place she could get a drink of water and bee lined toward the water fountain.

She wiped her chin and took a deep breath.

I can do this, she told herself.

Dealing with Anita was always particularly challenging but doing it with the headache from hell seemed impossible.

"Guess who's coming home," Anita started speaking before Chloe sat down.

"Who?"

"Abigail!" Anita could barely contain her excitement.

"To stay?"

"She doesn't realize it yet, but yes, she'll stay," Anita said confidently.

"But... why... how?"

"If you'd pick up the phone and call your sister every now and then you'd know that Todd left her. He's back home and he knocked up that Cathy Lang girl that Abigail went to high school with. That girl is trash and now Todd doesn't want anything to do with your sister or those two beautiful kids."

"What?" Chloe was stunned, her headache forgotten for the moment. "How is Abi?"

"You should reach out to her and see for yourself. Honestly, I don't know how I had two daughters that don't even speak to each other. I blame myself."

Chloe knew that wasn't true. Anita hadn't blamed herself for anything her entire life. She likely blamed Chloe.

"I'll reach out to her, Mom."

"Or... you could just see her when she gets home. She's coming on Friday for Daddy's birthday party on Saturday."

Chloe tried to hide her surprise. She hadn't seen Abi in six months and doubted she wanted to come back to the same place her lowlife ex would be living.

"What makes you think she wants to stay?" Chloe tried not to sound suspicious.

"Well, she doesn't know she wants to stay yet but I have a proposition for her if she does. Daddy and I are going to let her live with us for free and help pay for her to finish college." Anita sounded like she was announcing a contest winner, her voice bursting.

Chloe clamped her mouth closed.

When she was going to college the conversation had been very different, but she knew that if Anita paid for Abi's college, she would be indebted to her for quite some time.

Chloe felt a pang of guilt.

She hadn't reached out to Abi for months. Their lives had gone in two different directions and she had been too busy to check in on her. Their age distance made it difficult to connect. They were in two different places in their lives, but Chloe felt the failure deep in her bones. She hadn't done her job as a big sister. She was supposed to be there for Abi.

She'd promised her when she was young, when Anita and Anthony's drinking made them unbearable, that she would always look out for her but she'd forgotten.

She looked down at her watch. Only fifteen more minutes and then they could leave for lunch at the Cathead Diner, one of Savi's favorite places. She loved the kid's chicken fingers and Miss Jennifer that worked there.

Chloe had considered raising her to be a vegetarian, like she was, but Anita had ruined that at an early age.

At least at the Cathead, the noise would drown out some of Anita's talking and Chloe desperately needed her to stop.

"So, what do you think about that, Chloe?"

"About what? I didn't realize you'd asked me a question."

"What do you think about us letting Abi live with us and paying for college?"

"I think it's ... nice." Chloe came up with the best word she could think of without causing a war. College had always been a sore topic for them because her parents made her pay for all of hers after the academic scholarships with student loans. They hadn't contributed much, even though they had a lot, because they were saving for Anita's dream vacation to Europe that they never took.

It had only come up once in conversation, but it had been a doozy, and Chloe didn't talk to her parents for almost a year.

"Well, we would've paid more for your college because we were saving for retirement, but now we're in great shape so we can do more."

Chloe chomped down on her tongue until she swore she could taste blood. Her mother had a gift for revising history to fit her current needs.

"I have to go to the bathroom." Chloe stood up abruptly, her legs wobbly.

"Okay, but hurry. It's nearly time for lunch."

She walked to the bathroom and worried that her legs would give out.

I must be getting sick. She felt her forehead but it was cool and dry.

She hid out in the restroom with a cool paper towel on her forehead. She finally came out when she knew story time would be over.

"Mommy! Its time to go and see Miss Jennifer!" Savi had given

Magnolia Jane a big hug and run over to Chloe, excitedly. She loved lunches with Miss Jennifer at the Cathead after story time.

"Are you okay?" Anita looked at Chloe with genuine concern.

"Yes, I'm fine."

She felt her mother's eyes on her for a minute longer.

"Let's go." Chloe grabbed Savi's hand.

"Let's go, Nonny!" Savi grabbed Anita's hand with her free one, and the three of them made an awkward chain out of the library and across the street toward the Cathead Diner.

As Chloe walked in the door, she took in the familiar smells. She'd been coming here for years, and it always felt like home.

"Hi there!" Jennifer Wynn greeted them at the door. "How's my favorite little customer today?"

She tapped Savi on the nose and Savi beamed.

Jennifer Wynn had changed a lot throughout the year, and even though she and Chloe didn't know one another well, she felt strangely protective of her.

She had married Ryker Wynn a couple of years ago, and after his sister Maeve had her accident, Jennifer helped at the Cathead a couple of days a week.

Savi had taken a liking to her, even as a toddler, and they had a special connection that was evident every time they visited.

As Jennifer lead them to their seats, Chloe suddenly had the sensation that she was disappearing, and she realized that her vision was horribly blurred.

"Chloe, are you okay?" Anita stared at the horrified look on her daughter's face as she stood frozen in the middle of the busy dining room.

"Mom... something is wrong. Everything is really blurry." Chloe tried to push down the panic. She didn't want to upset Savi but she was frightened.

"What do you mean, your vision is blurry?"

"Blurry, Mom!"

"Has this ever happened before?" Jennifer's voice was full of concern.

"No! Never!"

"We're going to the ER." Anita grabbed Chloe's arm.

Chloe fought back tears and she allowed her mother and Jennifer to guide her. The warm salty breeze hit her face as they stepped outside, her hand tightly gripping Savi's.

"Mommy, I'm hungry." Savi cried, not understanding why they were suddenly leaving.

"I'll call your father and have him come and get you once we get to the hospital," Anita snapped.

Chloe tried to catch her breath. "He's out of town. You'll have to call and have him come back. He's only an hour away."

Chloe rubbed her eyes, desperately trying to clear her vision but it didn't work. Something was terribly wrong!

With horror, the thought took root in her mind that she was going to die.

6

Neena

Neena typed in the message and hit send before she could second-guess herself.

She waited, staring at the phone anxiously.

Sure, when? The response was almost immediate.

Tomorrow. Three o'clock. Our usual place? She typed, feeling guilty.

I'll see you then.

Neena loved the Cathead Diner and could definitely use a bowl of Maeve's Clam Chowder. She knew it would be a risk going to such a public place, but at five o'clock there was only a small chance that anyone would see them.

Especially her dad.

He always ate lunch early, and even though the Cathead was one of his favorite places, he likely wouldn't be there at that time.

After all, she would have to text him and see if she could drop Jaden off with him, but she knew he wouldn't ask questions. He trusted her implicitly. He would never imagine that she would lie to him.

But she couldn't tell him this.

She knew what he would say. He would tell her to stay away. He would tell her that she would only get hurt again and then he would get sad and she hated when he got sad. She hated being the source of any misery, but if she told him, she knew it would devastate him just like the last time.

It had been the two of them for as long as she could remember.

Then her mom had come back six years ago and Neena thought she might stay. It was the longest she could remember her sticking around and she began to get accustomed to her being around. Vanessa was home for a few months when she announced she was pregnant. As her stomach grew rounder, Neena became even more hopeful. If her mom wouldn't stay for her than maybe she would at least stay for the new baby.

Vanessa had missed most of Neena's childhood, always apologizing when she returned only to break their hearts once again.

Neena rubbed the scar on her chin where she had five stitches from falling down the porch steps when she was five. Daddy had spent all night with her in the emergency room, worried. It was the first time she had ever been hurt and she had never seen him so upset but he had comforted her. It was the first time in her life that she realized that it was just the two of them

Daddy and Neena.

Neena and Daddy.

Daddy had taken her to buy her first training bra, he had run out to buy supplies the first time she had her period, and had told her all about the birds and the bees.

When Vanessa left them again, shortly after Jaden was born, Neena promised Daddy that she would help him take care of her brother. He had been certain that his wife would stay this time and was devastated when she disappeared once again in the middle of the night.

"I'm so sorry! I thought for sure she was better and that she would stay this time." Daddy had held Neena, both of them heartbroken. "I can't keep doing this to you. To us. This time... it's over. I'm not going to let her keep hurting you."

He squeezed her tighter.

"It's okay, Daddy. You love her and I love her, too, but we have to protect Jaden now. I don't want her to hurt him like she's always done to me." Neena always surprised him with her maturity.

"You're a wonderful young woman, and you've become so strong, but I'm here for you. You'll never be alone, Neena. I'll make sure of it. Your mom has left you alone, but you never have to worry about that with me."

Neena pushed down the emotion that threatened to overcome her. He'd never said anything like that to her before and she knew he didn't realize it as he spoke to her deepest fear.

"It's going to be okay, baby girl. It's always just been you and me, and I'll take care of you. Everything is going be all right." His words reached deep down into her belly and gave her a peace she hadn't felt in years.

As her baby brother grew into an energetic, smiling ball of joy, Neena cared for him like he was her own. The residents of Grey's Harbor often mistook her for his mother, both admiring and judging her from afar, but Neena didn't care what they thought.

She loved him and was determined to protect him from everyone and everything.

She'd grown up in Grey's Harbor, always feeling like an outsider because she was different. She was the only mixed girl on the Harbor, her beautiful caramel skin and soft brown eyes the perfect compliment to her bouncy blonde ringlets that moved as vigorously as she did. She was keenly aware that she was different from most of the people she met, but she didn't give it much thought. As Jaden grew older, he began to resemble her more, and Daddy joked that he didn't look like him at all, only like his *Neens*.

Daddy and Neena were a team, raising Jaden together, allowing him to help heal their collective heartache as they missed the wife and mother they never had.

Neena lost herself in school, easily finding herself at the top of the class.

Daddy had insisted that Neena enroll in college classes at Grey's Harbor Community College. Her grades had earned her a scholarship and she was nearly finished with her nursing degree. The scholarship had been great, but the cost of her books caused them to struggle every semester.

She looked down at her phone and typed furiously.

Dad, I have a meeting tomorrow at three. Can you watch Little Man?

Sure! He responded quickly as he always did where she was concerned.

Her heart thumped as she thought about what she was going to do. He would be so disappointed in her, but she had to.

She couldn't say no.

Even though she wished it could be different, she was completely incapable of saying no.

She knew in the depth of her heart that this would always be her biggest downfall. Yet she just couldn't walk away.

Thank you, she texted. *Love you, Daddy.*

Love you, BG.

Neena ignored the sinking feeling in her gut.

❧ 7 ❧

G^{ina}

THE WORK PARTY WAS A SMASHING SUCCESS FOR THEO'S OFFICE, AND everybody remarked on how beautiful and fit his wife was after having two children.

Theo beamed, his hand around Gina's slim waist guiding her around the room like the doting husband that he was. His colleagues admired the obvious love between them.

Her shimmery dress clung to her long, lean frame. She clearly spent many hours in the gym, which made the women from his office feel self-conscious. Her bright smile was warm as she regarded those she was speaking to with the most remarkable green eyes anyone had ever seen.

Gina was the perfect hostess.

Their house was immaculate and beautifully decorated, and she hosted the party with the grace of a professional. The other wives observed with jealousy, though they disguised it under their fake lashes, false smiles, and well-painted faces.

"I can't wait to get you upstairs tonight and see what's under this dress," Theo whispered in Gina's ear.

Gina tried to disguise the shiver that ran through her.

She loved her husband. She admired his faithfulness and willingness to get on the floor and play with the kids, even in his suit after a long day. She was proud of how handsome he was and how his body still left her yearning, day after day. But she hadn't been feeling herself, and though she disguised it behind her perfect smile and warm eyes, she couldn't wait for everyone to leave so she could go to bed.

This was an important party, and she knew the impact it could have on Theo's career. Grey's Harbor's richest, most well-connected members of society were there, and she knew she had a part to play.

She had already spent time with the Greys, who she was surprised to genuinely like. Lillian and her daughter, Emerson were down-to-earth, and she could've spent all evening with them, but duty called. She reluctantly excused herself so she could mingle with the others, making a mental note to seek them out in the future.

She was happy to see that David Long was there.

She had met him a few times before and Theo talked about him often as someone he could rely on. He had a strange past with a college-aged daughter, toddler son, and an ex-wife with a history of addiction, and Theo admired that it never stood in the way of his ability to do his job. Gina looked over at him standing in the corner and felt a pang of sadness for him. He looked out of place in the room full of polished professionals. At six foot five, he already stood out in the crowd, and Theo said he refused to bring a date, which Gina thought was unfortunate since he was a decent-looking guy.

Strangely, she thought that Chloe's sister, Abi, might be a good match for him but dismissed the thought immediately. She was too young, and she hadn't even seen Abi since she left Grey's Harbor. According to Chloe, she barely heard from her sister these days, even after her lying husband cheated on her. Setting her up with David Long was out of the question.

She pushed away the slight dizziness that had been nagging at her all day.

She knew she hadn't been eating enough, which was likely part of the problem, but it required a lot of willpower to keep her slim figure. She had seen those pictures of herself after she'd given birth to Lincoln and Leo and she could barely even look at them.

Theo had made light of it. "You just did the most miraculous thing a person could do, Ginny. Why don't you give yourself a break? You're gorgeous no matter how much you weigh or what you look like."

Gina knew that Theo was just too generous. It was how he was built, raised by a mother who had the same nature. Neither one of them could see the bad in anyone, even though his father had been the opposite. Gina wished she could be like them, but her childhood had been completely different.

"There's no excuse to ever be fat." The memory of her mother slapping a cookie out of her hand suddenly appeared.

She looked down at her sleek waist and smiled. Who would even care if she had to purge dinner from last night and breakfast from this morning? It wasn't as though she did it as much anymore. She had learned to have better habits with food and only did it when the occasion arose.

She considered Theo's party a necessary occasion to look good for. She told herself she would eat a little extra over the next couple of days but looking perfect for him wasn't optional.

She wasn't sure how she had managed to find someone like Theo, but he had been smitten with her from day one in Psych 101 class in college and had never stopped. She knew she didn't deserve him but no matter what she did, he remained helplessly in love with her.

She even tested him early in their marriage, overspending on the credit cards, not cleaning the house, over cooking his eggs, but nothing she did could anger him. He was a rare human being, and she had come to accept that even though she didn't deserve him, he loved her beyond reason.

"So... What is under this dress?" Theo pulled her a little closer, his fingers pressing lightly through the thin material.

She wasn't in the mood to flirt. "It's nothing you haven't seen before," she said dismissively.

"I am going to want to see for myself anyway, if that's just the same to you," he whispered in her ear as he left a kiss on her earlobe.

Scotch made him flirty and Gina gave him a warning look.

"You have guests, darling."

"That doesn't matter. We could just go upstairs right now, and I could take your panties..."

"Theodore!" Gina said a little too loudly. She lowered her voice. "Stop it! We have guests who don't look like they're going to be leaving anytime soon."

Theo gave her his best puppy dog eyes and she relented, kissing him softly on the lips.

"You need to attend to your guests." She swiped gently at the lipstick she'd left behind.

As the evening wore on, people began to filter out. Gina was happy when the last guest left, all commenting on how perfect the night had been. Gina closed the door and flipped off her Jimmy Choos.

Theo swept her into his arms, his shirt already unbuttoned at the top, his well-muscled chest exposed.

"You, my beautiful girl, were a smashing success! God, I thought they'd never leave! I couldn't wait for them to go so I could take you upstairs and ravish you like you deserve!" Theo threw his arms in the air dramatically, as he bent over to kiss Gina.

Gina giggled in spite of herself. She was giddy with the success of the party and lost herself for a moment in the warmth of his lips, oaky from the Scotch.

"So, are you ready to do this?" He pulled her tight against him, his eyes crinkling as he smiled.

"You talk too much," Gina said kissing him again.

"Wait!" Theo lifted his head suddenly. "Did you eat tonight?"

Gina's stomach grumbled. She had been too busy to eat, only seltzer water throughout the night and a nibble on a piece of cheese.

She shook her head.

"I told you to make sure you ate tonight, Ginny. You never listen to me. I should've made you eat before the party. I knew you wouldn't do it!" Theo scolded her and tried his best to look angry. He grabbed her by the waist and ushered her into the kitchen.

She looked around the kitchen and tried not to get anxious about it as the staff from the catering company was busily cleaning.

"Everybody stop what you're doing!" Theo bellowed the top of his lungs.

The four women froze.

"My beautiful wife needs food, stat! We need to get her something, immediately! Which one of you wonderful women can help me out?"

The younger girl with the blonde hair and grey eyes hurried toward the fridge. "There are some lovely mini sandwiches here that weren't touched."

"Thank you so much." Theo's exuberance remained intact even though it was late in the evening.

Gina was embarrassed. Theo was the king of grand gestures, but she didn't want to be in the kitchen and in the way. She was always uncomfortable with hired help, even though Theo had been used to it his entire life.

Gina always felt like she should be working right next to them.

"Thank you so much, Jessie, isn't it?" Gina smiled graciously.

"Yes, ma'am." The girl smiled timidly, her eyes wide in surprise that Gina remembered her name.

Gina was struck at how beautiful she was, her beauty transformed by a simple smile.

"Did you happen to meet Gavin Grey tonight?" Gina asked Jessie.

"No, ma'am."

"Ahhh, that's too bad. He's quite a handsome young man, and he's your age. You might've hit it off."

Jessie blushed.

"Oh no, ma'am. He's way out of my league."

"No way! I don't believe in that!" Gina suddenly swayed as Theo grabbed her.

"Are you all right, Ginny?" His voice was immediately worried

"I'm fine." Gina reached out for a chair.

"Please sit and eat." Jessie took her hand and settled her at the breakfast bar. "I'll get some milk for you and you can eat as many of those sandwiches as you'd like."

"Oh, I don't wanna be any trouble," Gina said apologetically.

"Really, its fine. Its better you eat them and they don't go to waste."

Gina sat down at the breakfast bar and took a bite of her sandwich surprised at how delicious it was.

Suddenly, the room went black and she heard Jessie scream.

Theo ran to her side, but she had already hit the floor before he could catch her.

"Please! Call 911," Theo gestured frantically toward Jessie. "Something is terribly wrong with my wife!"

8

A^{bi}

"I WANT YOU TO COME HOME." MOM'S VOICE WAS CLEAR ON THE other end of the line, and Abi regretted answering the phone. She had been avoiding her calls since the first time she told her to come home.

She knew better.

"Daddy misses you and wants to see his grandbabies."

Abi knew it was coming, and she mentally checked herself for not being better prepared. She hadn't been home in almost a year, and while they had been to visit her, she couldn't bring herself to go back.

"Mom, it's just so hard to get away right now. I need to make money for the holidays." Abi knew her attempt to avoid visiting was weak and that her mother would see right through it.

"I don't want to hear that excuse, young lady. You've been avoiding us for months and I've let you have your time to mourn that pathetic relationship choice. But its time you face reality and just come home. I'm not saying you have to stay but you do need to visit... for awhile."

It was clear from her mother's voice that she was not going to take no for an answer.

Abi sighed.

"I'll have to..."

"You do what you need to do but I expect you to be here this weekend. Its Daddy's birthday and all he's been saying is that he wants to see you and his grandchildren. I'm not going to let you disappoint him. So, do whatever you need to, and we'll see you on Saturday."

Her mother hung up the phone before Abi could protest. She frantically started making arrangements to get rid of her shifts, and within an hour she was cleared for the next week and a half.

She lie back on the bed and put her hands on her head.

How did this happen? They had been so happy and then suddenly Todd was gone. He didn't even care about the kids any longer, which broke her heart. With his new baby in the way, he seemed to have forgotten that he already had two kids that called him daddy.

"Why doesn't Daddy tuck us in anymore?" Lexi asked. At eight years old, she was growing up so fast, and Abi was stunned at how much she reminded her of Chloe.

Abi sighed. She wanted to be honest but didn't want to break her heart with his bad choices.

"It's not your fault, sweetheart. Grown ups can be dumb sometimes, too." Abi had kissed her on top of her soft forehead and stayed with her until she had fallen asleep.

As she watched Lexi sleep, she thought about how she had fallen in love with Todd when they were just fifteen. He was a local boy whose daddy was a fisherman. They had lived in the south side, in a ramshackle home that sometimes had electricity and sometimes didn't.

It had just been Todd and his dad, and no matter how hard she tried, Abi could never get him to tell her what happened to his mom.

He never had any intention of leaving Grey's Harbor, but he'd followed a job that he promised her would make good money, so against her parents wishes, she'd followed him.

It was the first time she'd ever disobeyed her parents and she'd felt guilty about it. They had been upset, but they couldn't stop her no matter how much they yelled or threatened her. Eventually they came around, but it wasn't until Lexi was born and they wanted to see her.

Now she would have to return home and admit that she had made a horrible mistake. She had no doubt in her mind by now that the whole town knew and that her parents would've been embarrassed. She pictured Daddy stopping to get his haircut at Manny's. Manny was a second cousin of Todd's and Daddy would've been embarrassed, but he liked Manny and would never think about going anywhere else.

Mom at her book club meeting in the Grey's Harbor Library would certainly be asked questions about when her youngest daughter would be returning now that her loser-husband had impregnated someone else.

Worst of all, she knew she would have to face Chloe.

Sometimes a mother and sometimes a sister, Chloe hadn't said anything about what was happening. Abi assumed she was too busy getting promoted and driving her expensive car to care what was happening in her pathetic life.

Truthfully, Abi was disappointed that Chloe didn't have anything to say in the matter. She would've expected her to have a strong opinion about her life, as she usually did. After all, she had told Abi just to fuck him, not to marry him.

Abi hadn't listened and had gotten pregnant, convinced she was in love.

Now she would have to divorce him, and divorces were expensive. She knew he would never pay for it.

She also knew that going home meant she would run into him. The Harbor was small, and he would likely be going to all of the same places she would end up in.

Going home to visit also meant her parents would want her to stay.

"There's no point in living so far from home now! Why would you struggle when you could just come home, go back to college, and let Daddy and I help you with our grandbabies?" Anita had never understood Abi's need for independence. While they had always been sweet to Lexi and Dom, she didn't want them to experience the crushing disappointment of being Anita and Anthony's offspring when they lived there full-time like she and Chloe had.

Still, she couldn't ignore the ache in her feet and the exhaustion that reflected in the dark circles under her eyes from lack of sleep. She longed for the days when her mom would make her breakfast and she could just go to school without any other pressure.

But this is being an adult, she reminded herself. She was a mother now and couldn't rely on her own mom to baby her anymore. Even though their five-bedroom house had plenty of space and no one to fill it, she was afraid that if she went home she'd never leave again.

"That's a nice offer, Mom." Abi had been careful with her words. "But I need to be able to take care of my babies on my own. I need to know that I can."

"But why would you do that to yourself and to them when you can make it so much easier on yourself? You've always done things the hard way! Don't make this so much harder than it needs to be!"

Abi had spent summers hostessing at the Cathead and knew that Maeve would always have her back in a heartbeat, but she didn't want that. She had fought to become a woman in the short six months since Todd had left. Even though it had been hard, she was finally paying her own bills and putting food on the table for the kids all by herself.

Her mother was right about one thing.

Abi was set on doing everything on her own and had been even from a young age. She would sit and try to tie her shoes for hours without accepting help. At five, she broke her arm because she refused to let Chloe hold her hand the first time she went on roller skates. Then Chloe had been grounded for a month, which Abi had felt bad about.

Abi knew she had a stubborn streak, but it didn't diminish the fact that she wanted to be able to take care of her own kids without anyone's help.

Still...

She opened her closet and started to pull random clothes off of hangers.

Riley, the black and brown mutt that she and Todd had rescued as a puppy three years before, stared up at her from the bed, curious.

"You're going to meet your grandparents," Abi told her, kissing her on the snout. She hadn't even told her mom about the dog, but it was too late now. She was going to take her home, too.

She tried to ignore the ball in the pit of her stomach that reminded her how nervous she was about going home.

It's just for a weekend, she reminded herself. She started to make a mental list of all the things she would need to pack.

She looked at the pile of clothes she had thrown on the bed and realized it was far more than she would ever need for a weekend.

She tried to quiet the voices in her head that told her she would be gone far longer even though she fought against it with everything inside of her.

She looked around her tiny bedroom and felt a sense of grief wash over her.

She refused to admit it out loud, but she realized that she was leaving her apartment forever and would likely not return.

9

C hloe

IT HAD ALREADY BEEN A LONG DAY, AND THE HOSPITAL ADMITTED Chloe for further observation and tests.

It had been several years since Chloe had been to the doctor for herself. Savi had been her priority but she had neglected to take care of herself, insisting that if she felt fine she was healthy. With her job and taking care of the house, she was far too busy to sit around a doctor's office waiting to be told she was fine.

But now, Chloe was subjected to tests that she never even knew existed. She remembered why she had neglected to go to the doctor for all of those years. She hated being poked and prodded, even though she knew it was necessary.

"I'm okay, Mom. You can go home now." Chloe had insisted, but Anita refused to take 'no' for an answer and was ready to battle her eldest daughter.

"You're clearly not okay, Chloe. You can't see properly." Anita was used to Chloe's stubbornness. "You need to finish this until they find out what's wrong with you!"

Anita insisted that her own doctor oversee Chloe's case, and Chloe was too shaken and tired to argue with her.

As they sat in the hospital room and waited for the results Anita to tried fill the space with small talk, ignoring Chloe's lack of interest in having any conversation.

"You know your sister will be home tomorrow, and she's excited to see you." Anita stared at Chloe, waiting for a response.

"Did Abi actually say that?" Chloe asked, doubtful.

"No. She didn't say that she was excited to see you specifically, but I know her." Anita had a way of reading peoples minds that was rarely accurate but liked to share it as though it were the truth.

Anita's incessant talking was making Chloe's head pound even worse. She was annoyed that she was missing another day of work to go through a bunch of tests that were only going to tell her that she was stressed out. She had been telling Brent that she needed a vacation, and they had agreed that the headaches and fatigue were stress induced.

Brent had no choice but to cancel his trip when Chloe was taken to the E.R. He picked Savi up from the hospital and took her home, where Anita insisted he remain while she looked after Chloe. Brent had learned it best not to argue with Anita when she had her mind made up about something.

Anita had always scared him.

"I'll come up later," he had conceded, wondering how pissed Chloe must be at him for leaving her with her mother, although, he knew it would be impossible for her to be any angrier with him than she already was.

Anita's doctor entered the room with Chloe's chart in his hands. He didn't say a word as he flipped through the file, and Chloe wondered if he'd even read it before he walked into the room.

After a few long moments, Anita cleared her throat loudly.

Dr. Reid looked up from the file as though realizing they were in the room for the first time. "Oh, hello, Mrs. Driver. Its good to see you again. This must be the patient, Chloe?"

Chloe nodded, trying to disguise her amusement. His jacket had a hole in the pocket and his curly hair was unruly and needed to be combed down.

"So, doc. Tell us about my girl here. What is wrong with her?"

"You're always straight to the point." Dr. Reid's expression was serious. He pushed up his wire rim glasses and sighed.

"Does cancer run in your family?" Dr. Reid stared at both of them, unblinking, his eyes lingering longer on Chloe. She squirmed in her seat, the room suddenly very warm.

"Not that I'm aware," Anita said her voice taking on an edge.

"Why did you ask?" Chloe fought the urge to run out of the room.

"I have some rather bad news. According to the MRI of your brain, you have a rather large tumor. Based on your symptoms, possibly a meningioma." He showed where it was and what it looked like, and as he continued to talk she couldn't concentrate.

Tumor.

Chloe heard the words brain, and tumor and felt as though all of the air had been sucked from the room. "Excuse me? I have a what?"

"I'm afraid it's rather sizable. Your last eye exam showed a slight amount of pressure behind your right eye. Did anybody ever tell you that?"

"I don't... Maybe... I don't remember." Chloe searched for the memory of her last eye exam and came up blank. It had to have been when Savi was just learning how to walk, and Chloe had been distracted.

"That is impossible! My daughter can't have a brain tumor! We don't have any cancer in our family, she's never smoked, and she's ridiculously healthy. She doesn't even eat meat for God's sake." Anita's voice was on the verge of hysteria and Chloe shot her a warning look.

"Mom!"

Dr. Reid ignored Anita's outburst. Chloe was sure he would have dealt with some doozies over the years.

"Meningiomas aren't often cancerous but can be dangerous. We won't know until it's removed and a biopsy is done."

"Removed?" Chloe thought Anita might faint.

"I'm sending you to an oncologist. She's one of the best and is right here in the Harbor. You may have to go to Gilmore General for some of your treatments, but that's for the best."

Chloe's head was spinning, and she wasn't sure if it was from the information he'd just given her, or because of her pounding head. She was sleepy from the medication they had her on, but it wasn't touching the pain.

"So, am I going to die?" Chloe blurted our before she could stop herself.

Dr. Reid looked her in the eye.

"We're all going to die." His voice was even. "See the oncologist, let her treat you, and see what happens."

Chloe tried to still her pounding heart as she stared at Anita who sat motionless in the chair next to her bed.

Dr. Reid continued to talk but she could no longer listen to or focus on anything he said.

It wasn't fair that this would happen to her. She'd already been through so much. She shouldn't have to go through this, too.

Anita finally found her voice.

"We'll get through this, together." Anita looked at Dr. Reid. "I'll take care of my girl. She'll be fine."

Chloe closed her eyes and fought back the tears.

Anita was best in a crisis. She lived for it; she always had, but Chloe knew what would happen next. Her tumor was no longer going to be about her. Now it was about Anita, and as long as she was going through this, it would continue to be.

She wondered if she would live to see Savi grow up, and she let the tears flow as she allowed herself to think she might not. She hadn't lived the life she had wanted to, and she knew it. Until now, she had accepted it, but suddenly she was desperate to live the life she'd only ever imagined.

But now she might not ever get to do that.

The one person in her life who could help her do that was gone for good. He was the only one she wanted to live her life with, and he had left her a long time ago.

Damn you, Linc.

Angry tears ran down her cheeks as she turned her head away from her mother.

Damn you.

eena

"You didn't bring the boy?"

Neena sipped her coffee, slowly, savoring its roasty richness.

The Cathead Diner always had the best coffee.

"No, I wouldn't bring him to see you!"

"But I was looking forward to it."

"I'm sorry, but until I saw what this was all about, I wasn't going to bring him." Neena had promised Jaden that she would always protect him.

Her daddy had done his best to keep her far from the demons, but his belief that people could change had exposed her to so much pain. He was kind and loved with his entire heart, but he was naive.

She wasn't going to do that to Jaden.

"I'm sorry you feel like you need to protect him from me, but I'm not a monster."

Neena felt a twinge of guilt, but she reminded herself why she had to protect him.

"Momma, I didn't say you're a monster. I just said that I needed to see what was going on." Neena had been surprised when Vanessa had walked through the door that she looked relatively healthy.

The last time she'd seen her was two years before and she had been a mess then. At least she'd put on a couple of pounds and looked like she'd been at least attempting to take care of herself.

Neena had seen many pictures of her parents in better days. They had been a beautiful couple. Vanessa was gorgeous all on her own, her caramel skin luminous, her brown eyes soft and shining. She was tiny in comparison to Neena's daddy, David. He was six five with blond hair and blue eyes that shined when he looked at his wife.

Neena had a vague memory of that.

But Neena didn't know that version of her mother from photos. She was only familiar with her real-life counterpart; ragged and worn out.

Vanessa gave her a disapproving look that made Neena squirm. Vanessa had a way of making Neena feel as though she was five years old, even though she'd never been much of a mother at all. She had left her with a daddy who had no idea how to raise a little girl on his own.

"So where have you been?" Neena asked, unable to stop. She had told herself she would wait until Vanessa volunteered the information. She didn't want to look too eager as though she had missed her too much, but she had.

She had missed her intensely, and it had been this way her entire life. Vanessa's absence always sat in the back of her mind, a constant distraction from the present. She always felt as though a piece of herself was somewhere else in the world, living a life she wanted desperately to be a part of.

"You know, doll. I've been a little bit of here, and a little bit of there." Vanessa played with the sugar packets on the table, refusing to make eye contact.

Neena looked at the tiny woman sitting in front of her and grief washed over her. This woman had carried her in her body for eight months, creating her from nothing but love.

"We were happy then," Daddy had told her many times throughout her childhood. "Even if it didn't last, we did love each other when we created you."

But the desire for every high was too strong, and Vanessa had been too weak to fight it. It had been a battle she waged all of her life, and her mom and daddy before her. Even before she met David and had Neena, she struggled.

She thought she had it licked but she couldn't escape her past or future, and she was never too particular about the flavor of her drug.

It didn't matter if she had to snort, shoot, swallow or inhale it. If it took her mind, and the memories away, she was in.

Even being Neena's momma didn't take the hunger away.

"Seriously, Momma, where have you been?" Neena had always let her get away with not answering the question, but she knew that she was risking too much to take chances this time.

"I said, doll. I've been here and there. I don't owe you anything. I'm a grown woman and I don't answer to you." Her tone was hard and one Neena recognized well.

She tried to picture Vanessa as a young woman, the remnants of that once breathtaking girl hard to see in the mask of the addict sitting in front of her. Vanessa was trying really hard not to look like one at the moment, but Neena recognized her.

She'd learned how to over the years.

"So, what do you want from me this time?" Neena made her voice as hard as Vanessa's had been.

"Oh, doll!" Vanessa laughed, trying to lighten the mood. "I just wanted to see you and my baby boy, but you didn't bring him."

"There has never been a time when *you just wanted to see me.*" Neena reminded herself who she was dealing with. No matter how strong the desire was to crawl into the booth next to her mother and beg her to hold her with her bony arms, she knew she couldn't give in.

Vanessa wanted something. She always did.

She had seen her daddy do it too many times to count, only to be to left with his heart broken. Neena wasn't going let her do that to her again.

"Oh, you're so smart, now that you're a college girl? Do you think you're smarter than your momma?" Vanessa's dark eyes blazed, and for a moment Neena thought she was going to reach across the table and slap her.

This was the mother she remembered. The short temper and the sharp tongue. The hand that came out of nowhere to slap her for the slightest offense.

Vanessa always loved her, until she didn't, and then would take off, chasing her next high.

The patterns were always the same.

"I said I just wanted to see you and my boy. I know I've fucked up too many times and there's no reason for you to believe me, but it's the truth." Her charcoal eyes look down at the table as she used the remnant of her fingernail to scrape at a clean place in the table.

"I'm sorry, Momma. You have to understand that I'm very protective of him, and I have to do everything in my power to make sure that Jaden doesn't have the same kind of childhood I did with you." Neena knew the words would sting the moment they left her mouth, but it had to be said.

Just then a pretty waitress with dishwater blonde hair approached the table. "Would you like some coffee?" she asked, holding up a steaming pot.

Neena nodded, grateful for the interruption

"Should we order?" Neena grabbed a menu off the table and opened it.

"I'm not hungry much, but if you'd like to eat go right ahead."

Even though Vanessa had put on a couple of pounds, she still had a long way to go.

"Come on, Momma. Order something."

Vanessa stubbornly slammed her hand down. "If I was hungry, I'd order something, damnit! Quit tryin' to make me do something I don't wanna do!"

The waitress backed slowly away as Neena mouthed "sorry."

"What do you want with me, Momma? Why are you here this time?" Neena tried to hide her frustration.

"I said... I just wanted to see you, doll. That's it."

"Then eat lunch with me," Neena insisted. "You used to love it here. This used to be one of your favorite places."

"I don't remember that." Vanessa's eyes darted around the restaurant as though she was seeing it for the first time. "I don't remember much about some things."

Neena tried to ignore the pit in her stomach. She averted her eyes so she wouldn't stare at Vanessa's rotting teeth.

Neena wondered if they hurt and how many she had lost. She knew it had to be uncomfortable for her to eat now, but she wanted to do something to help her momma who seemed so far out of reach. She felt her eyes beginning to well over and she stood up abruptly.

"I've got to go to the bathroom. The coffee is running right through me." Neena wiped her eyes quickly so Vanessa couldn't see. "Do you want to come?"

"I don't need to babysit you while you piss."

Neena tried to ignore the crassness of her comment.

"OK, I'll be right back." She rushed to the bathroom and prayed the tears would wait.

She thought she would be able to handle it by herself but now she wasn't sure. She didn't want to cry in front of Vanessa and let her see how much she'd hurt her. She wanted Vanessa to see she hadn't needed her after all.

As she swiped at her eyes in front of the mirror, she realized with sudden horror that she had made the biggest mistake.

Instead of grabbing her purse to go to the restroom, she had left it in the booth with Vanessa.

In her wallet was the cash she'd been saving for all of her textbooks. She ran out of the bathroom as fast as she could. But as she stood in the middle of the dining room, her heart sank.

The booth she'd been sitting in with Vanessa was now completely empty. As she got closer, she realized that everything was gone.

Everything.

11

G ina

GINA OPENED HER EYES.

She had only been out for a few minutes but it felt like much longer.

"Call 911!" Theo was repeating.

"I don't want an ambulance, Theo!" Gina tried to sit up, embarrassed to realize she was on the ground with everyone staring at her.

"Really, you should go. I insist. You haven't been yourself for the last couple of weeks and something could be wrong," Theo pleaded with her.

"I know what's wrong. I don't need to go to the hospital," Gina insisted.

"It's not a normal thing to pass out."

"Yeah, well it is when you're pregnant," Gina said her voice tired.

Theo's dark eyes widened in surprise.

"You're pregnant?" Theo's face twisted in confusion. "But... I had a vasectomy. I mean... how did this happen?"

"The doctor said it happens. We might've had sex too early... or the procedure failed... either way. I'm pregnant."

Theo looked at her gravely. "But..."

"It's fine... "

"You know what happened..."

"Theo, please stop talking." Gina looked at the catering crew and gave him a warning look. They took her cue and left the room without a word.

Gina didn't want to be pregnant.

She hated the thought of starting all over with shitty diapers and all nighters. She had just gotten her body back to where it had been before Lincoln and Leo has wreaked havoc on her. She had even agreed to a breast augmentation because they thought they were done having children. She mourned the impending loss of her slim figure.

More than that, she was terrified about the pregnancy itself. They had advised her when Leo was born that it might not be safe for her to have any more children, which was why Gina and Theo agreed that he should get the vasectomy.

She pushed the thought out of her mind.

It would different this time. She had to believe it.

At eight weeks, Gina had wrestled with the knowledge that she was growing another human, alone. She had considered aborting without Theo's knowledge, but she couldn't bring herself to. She thought about Lincoln and Leo and how much she adored them and couldn't imagine killing her own child.

Part of her was angry with Theo for wanting to play nurse and doctor, one of his favorite role-plays, so soon after the vasectomy without any other protection. "It'll be fine, baby." Theo had breathed heavily in her ear as he thrust inside of her from behind. "I can't get you pregnant now. So just enjoy what the doctor is giving you."

But here she was, knocked up like a sixteen-year-old schoolgirl who didn't know any better.

"When were you going to tell me?" Theo looked at her, somberly. "How long have you known?"

"I've known for a couple of weeks now." Gina's voice could barely be heard.

"When were you going to tell me?" Theo's usually calm demeanor was rattled.

"I-I-I don't know when I was going to tell you. I was trying to figure it out for myself."

"Figure what out for yourself?" Theo tried to control his voice.

"I don't know what I was trying to figure out. I was just lost." Gina looked ashamed, the tears brimming in her deep blue eyes.

"Aren't we supposed to be in this together, you and me? I can't support you if you don't let me." Theo pulled her off the floor and made her sit in a chair while he poured her a glass of water.

"I know." Gina refused to meet his stare. She had learned early in her life not to ask for things and it had carried over into her marriage.

"So, what are we going to do? Are you happy at all? Is this safe?" Theo wasn't sure what to do with all of the emotions flowing through him.

"I don't know, Theo. I … didn't want one. Neither did you. That's why you had the vasectomy!" Gina said without thinking.

"I know, but … now that it's here… do you feel any differently?"

Gina stared at Theo's handsome face. He'd only had the vasectomy because she'd begged him to. If it were up to him, he would have ten kids, but after the doctor advised her not to have any more, she was more than happy to oblige.

She'd always struggled to be a mother even though she never let it show. Keeping the house together after two small children that had no respect for the hours she spent cleaning was exhausting. Still she did it because that was her job, and even though she'd never said it out loud, sometimes she hated her job.

She was ashamed of not wanting more children

The thought of her empty canvases popped into her head again. She shook her head as though to make them disappear, but they had a habit of invading her thoughts at the worst possible moment. She had plans before she met Theo. She was smart and creative and was going to be an artist. She knew she was a damn good one because every teacher she ever had told her so. When she met Theo, all of that promise was wiped out with a plus sign on a pregnancy test.

She put them away in their big spacious attic and refused to look at them again but now they haunted her like a ghost.

"Is this even safe?" Theo suddenly remembered what the doctor had advised.

"They said they would monitor me closely." Gina sighed.

"Aren't you even a little happy about this?" Theo searched her eyes.

"No, I don't want another baby, Theo. I'm sorry. But it doesn't matter what *I* want. I'm pregnant and we can't undo that now. Nobody ever cares what I want, do they? Don't we think that having two little monsters is enough?" Hearing the words out loud made it even worse, but Gina couldn't stop herself.

"I don't know what to say." Theo looked like a balloon that had been deflated of all of its air. "I thought we were happy. I thought you were happy. I didn't know that you resented being a mother so much."

"It's not that I resent being a mother, but you have no idea how much I've struggled. As long as things have been perfect for you, which I've made damn sure they have, you didn't care about me at all."

"That's not true!" Theo tried to control his voice. He had never yelled at a woman, but Gina was being unfair. He had spent their entire marriage caring about her happiness, bringing her flowers and buying her jewelry and telling her how beautiful she was.

She was the most beautiful woman Theo had ever seen and it didn't matter if she was plump with pregnancy or fit as a rail, he only saw his beautiful, capable wife.

"So, what do we do now?" Theo asked, fighting the urge to pull Gina into his arms.

"I don't know." Gina was already resigned to surrender to the tiny life that was invading her body.

"Are we okay?" Theo was afraid to say the words out loud.

"You're okay." Gina stared up at her husband, mortified by what she had done. She had never wanted him to know her secret misery. He was a good man and she loved him and adored their children, but some days she felt as though motherhood was a mask that she had to take on and off.

"I'm sorry," Gina finally said laying her head against Theo's shoulder and he drew her in closer to him.

"No, I'm sorry," he murmured in her ear. "I'm sorry you've felt so alone. I know I should've been more aware because I know what you went through when you were a child. You just hide everything so well that I thought you were okay. I'm just a stupid man and I'm sorry." Gina closed her eyes and pushed down the enormous sob that was threatening to erupt from her chest.

Theo and the boys had taught her how to love, but it still felt unnatural, her entire life fighting the pain after her brother left and everything before that.

"Everything is going to be okay, and I'll take care of you." Theo felt his promise with every bone in his body.

Gina hated her selfishness and did as she had her entire life. She squared her shoulders and told herself she would get through it. She put her hand on her stomach and fought the nausea that never seemed to go away with this pregnancy.

I can do this she told herself.

She willed away the dread that lurked just below the surface like a black cloud, waiting to take her soul.

12

A bi

WITH EVERY MILE, AS ABI AND THE KIDS GOT CLOSER TO GREY'S Harbor, her heart pounded faster and harder in her chest.

She knew as soon as she arrived that her life would no longer be her own. Perhaps that wasn't such a bad thing, since she had screwed it up so much. She was so sure when she had left with Todd that she would never be back, except for the occasional visit.

She was confident that she'd never again have to deal with her mother's overbearing opinion of everything she'd ever screwed up in life. Or even Chloe's jealousy because for some strange reason she thought Abi was the favorite even though there was nothing farther from the truth.

Now, she would have to return to the Harbor with her tail tucked between her legs, and likely run into Todd and that whore, Cat.

Her hands gripped the steering wheel until her knuckles were white.

"She's my soul mate," he had said, his tone suggesting that it was a perfectly acceptable reason to abandon them. "I'm sorry, Abi, but you wouldn't want me to stay with you knowing that we weren't soul mates, would you?"

"It wasn't my fault," Abi muttered under her breath, careful not to wake the kids who were sleeping in the back

"What wasn't your fault, Mommy?" Lexi asked. Abi could see her rubbing her eyes in the rear-view mirror.

"I'm sorry, baby. I didn't mean to wake you." Abi smiled.

"But what wasn't, Mommy?"

"It's nothing, baby. Mommy was just thinking out loud." Abi was always careful not to share her thoughts with the kids. They were too young and her thoughts were often too dark. She wanted them to have good memories of a happy childhood, unlike her own. She hated Todd for scarring them as she thought about the many nights they'd cried themselves to sleep as they asked for him.

"Are you excited about seeing Nonny?" Lexi asked her brother, Dom, who had just woken up.

"No! I want to go home." Dom buried his hands in Riley's soft fur and laid his head on her large body that draped across him. He was always crabby when he woke up, but especially now. He hadn't wanted to leave.

I want to go home too, kiddo.

Abby wanted to say it out loud but knew she couldn't. She had to make the kids think this was the best thing they'd ever done.

She imagined what would happen as soon as they stepped into her parent's house and pictured herself immediately transformed into a child.

Her mom had never seen her as a woman, even after she was married with two children. In her eyes she was always the baby, and Abi wanted more than that. She wanted to be like Chloe, where her mother saw her as a strong and capable woman instead of a little girl.

Her parents offered many times to let them live in their house indefinitely, rent free, since Todd had left but she had refused.

"I insist," her mom had said on the phone in her don't argue with me, tone.

She had always hung up before making a commitment, but her mom was wearing her down.

Deep down, Abi knew it was the best thing for her and the children. They had still not been able to put down roots because Todd moved them every year or so for a new job, always dissatisfied with the job he had.

As much as she wanted to do it alone, she knew it would be better for the children if their lives were more stable. Even though her parents could be overbearing, at least they had always provided that, and Abi knew they had mellowed over the years. She was more prepared to shield them than she was able to protect herself as a child

She was eager but afraid to hear what Chloe would say, even though she hadn't spoken to her sister in months. Their adult relationship had a strange ebb and flow that brought them together and pulled them apart without any rhyme or reason.

She knew Chloe would think she was ridiculous for coming back home. She'd always told Abi how proud she was of her for leaving home.

"I don't know why you want us to move home so badly when you have Chloe and Savi here, too. We'll just be in your way." Abi knew it was a lame attempt to get her mother to let her off the hook.

"That's the silliest thing I've ever heard. Chloe and Savi don't even live with us," her mom said, dismissing it without a thought.

"Savi will love getting to know her cousins. She doesn't really even know them since you've been away." Abi's mom knew how to lay on the guilt, one of the many skills she always used to her advantage.

As Abi made the mindless drive to Grey's Harbor, she tried to ignore the sense of her dwindling freedom.

She knew her mom would take control of every aspect of her life if she could. For a split second she thought about asking Chloe if she could stay with her, but she erased that thought from her mind as soon as it came.

Sisterhood couldn't be forced and as much as she wanted it, their mom had done a lot to prevent them from being close.

Abi thought about all the things she had left behind in her apartment that she would need to go back and get. Although Todd had taken a lot of the things that cost the most money, she still had a couch that she loved and other things she had accumulated along the way.

The kids would be thrilled to sleep on real beds. They had been sleeping on a mattress on the floor of their bedroom because they couldn't afford to get them a bed. It seemed so much more important to buy food than to buy a box spring and a bed frame, but now Abby wondered if buying a bed for them had been the most important thing and she had missed it.

She'd followed Todd to a city where she knew no one and anywhere else he had decided to go, yet she was reluctant to follow him home.

In the beginning their love had been exciting and fun. While he had never been the perfect, most attentive boyfriend, Abi tried to imagine now what had attracted her to him so much. He had been her first, in every way, and she had never questioned whether there was better than him.

"I love you, baby. You're the only one for me," he'd told her as he pushed her hair back behind her ears. She had loved him for always doing that, and no matter what else he did, if he did that, she felt safe.

Even after the kids were born, she told herself that she had a good life. All young couples were stretched for money. All young families struggled. Now she wondered if that was true or if his words had just taken root inside of her so that she wouldn't know any better.

Abi knew that going home was the best thing for the kids, but she wasn't sure that going home was the best thing for her. She wanted stability, but she yearned for independence. When she thought about how the late hours, her tired feet, and the stress of constantly finding a babysitter wore her to the bone, she knew she couldn't do it alone for much longer.

She needed help.

Todd had promised her freedom and now she had nothing. She wondered if Chloe would've ever put up with someone like Todd, then thought it was foolish of her to even wonder that since Chloe had such a perfect life. Everything Chloe had worked for she had achieved at a young age.

Chloe had always been very driven and never accepted 'no' for an answer from anyone. It was why she and their mom could be at war so often, both fighting to be on top. Abi had never understood how the two of them could clash so much. Abi knew that if Chloe just let her mom have her way that it made everything easier.

"Only sixty-eight miles until Grey's Harbor," Abi said to no one in particular. Both children, and Riley, had fallen back to sleep in the backseat of the car. Butterflies fluttered in her stomach and she felt as though she could barely breathe.

She rolled down her window and breathed in that smell. It had been a long time since the smell of the sea had invaded her nose and somehow it made her feel calm.

She hated to admit how much she had missed it all.

The salty smell instantly brought back a thousand memories, most of them good. It was the one thing she knew she would be happy to see.

And as much as she hated to admit it, she would be happy to see her mom, but deep down she knew she'd never leave again.

❧ 13 ❧

C hloe

"I can't believe this is happening!"

Chloe could hear the agony in her best friend's voice on the other end of the line. "How... why... I mean... God. I don't know what I mean. What's going to happen, Chlo?"

"I don't know yet, but I have to see the oncologist and we'll make a plan then. I don't even know if it's operable ... or how bad it is yet." Chloe couldn't believe she was talking about a tumor.

In her head.

It felt as though she was talking about someone else. She'd heard of people having brain tumors, but she'd never known anyone personally or even considered that she might ever have one. Cancer didn't run in her family and she had always tried her best to live a healthy lifestyle. It was surreal.

She felt ridiculously unprepared and hated that more than anything.

"So ... what does Anita say about all of this?"

"What do you think she said? She said that it's going to be fine and that I'll get through this. In the meantime, she's absolutely devastated and it's all about her." Chloe laughed at the irony.

She knew that Gina would understand better than anyone.

They'd been friends for a long time, growing up right next to each other, both trapped in their own private hell without the other knowing.

Gina had it worse though, and Chloe knew it. Chloe's parents had never put cigarettes out on her skin or kept her out of school for weeks at a time while her bruises healed like Gina's had.

Chloe's parents weren't addicts or alcoholics who would do absolutely anything to get their next high, even when it hurt their own children. On the outside, Gina's childhood looked like everyone else's on the street, until it all finally fell apart. After Linc abruptly disappeared from Grey's Harbor, neither Chloe nor Gina were ever the same.

Gina had lost her brother and Chloe had lost her first love. The pair had already become tight but without Linc, they became like sisters. Even after Gina moved in with her aunt and uncle in Gilmore, they still talked every day, the bond between them remaining strong.

Gina never trusted anyone again until she finally gave her heart to Theo, the first man to know close to everything about her and love her just the same. He moved them to a big beautiful house on the coastal side of Grey's Harbor and promised her a good life, but that didn't change who she was when she looked in the mirror.

Both women had been hard-working in school, Chloe more academic while Gina had been artsy. Chloe never understood why Gina hadn't pursued her love of painting and always tried to encourage her, but Gina had insisted she was happy.

When Chloe went for her MBA, Gina had helped her with Savi when Brent was working. She even understood Chloe's mother and how she drove her crazy but compared to her own mother, Anita had been a saint. Yet Gina understood Chloe in every way and could still see all of the cracks and fissures in her soul created by the pressure to be the perfect daughter, wife, mother, and professional.

Gina had an artist's eye for every detail, so she saw things that nobody else did.

She always had

"Are you okay?" Chloe knew the answer before she asked. She was Gina's only family and the thought of leaving her alone made her heart ache.

There was silence.

"Gina? Are you there?" Chloe spoke louder.

"I'm here. "Gina's response was muffled, and Chloe knew she was trying to hide her tears. She kicked herself mentally for not telling her in person, but she wanted her to know.

"What are we going to do?"

"I don't know. I don't want to think about it." Chloe took a ragged breath. She was already exhausted from thinking about it and she knew it was just beginning.

She had persuaded Brent to take Savi for ice cream so she could have some quiet time at home. Anita has been near hysterics but insisted that she could drive herself home after dropping Chloe off. Chloe needed to decompress like she usually did after spending too much time with her mother.

She was exhausted and happy to finally be home after being released. Her eyesight was still blurry but she was getting used to it. She was allowed to go home under the condition that she stay there until her doctor appointments.

"What does Brent say?" Gina asked cautiously.

"Brent and I haven't even had a chance to talk. I don't know what he's going to say. I don't know if this is going to change anything between us."

"Is he staying at the house?"

"For now." Chloe rubbed her temple. "He's going to stay here in the guest bedroom until we figure out what's going on. I thought we might be able to work it out, but now there's no point in him moving out if ..."

"Don't even say it!" Gina demanded. "I know what you're about to say, and don't even think about it. We're going to get through this. Brent can do whatever he wants to do, but we are going to get through this."

"I don't even want him here, but Savi needs him."

"And you? Do you need him?"

"I haven't needed him for a long time, but Anita insisted that I give him another chance. I can't stand looking at him when I know he just wants to be with her." Chloe tried to ignore the sharp pain in her heart as she said the words out loud.

"Then why don't you and Savi just come and stay with me? You don't need him there, so kick him out and come stay with us."

"Don't you already have enough to worry about?" Chloe said pointedly.

Gina had texted her about her fight with Theo. It was rare that Gina and Theo fought about anything, but this had been a big one. Chloe knew how miserable her friend had been, but she refused to talk to Theo about it. Chloe also knew that Theo would do anything to make Gina happy, but Gina had to figure that out for herself.

"This is more important." Chloe could hear the stubbornness in Gina's voice.

She knew that Gina would insist that they come stay with her but she needed to sleep in her own bed. Even if that meant that Brent would be nearby in the guest bedroom.

"Thank you, but Savi needs to be at home right now. If things change, I will come and stay with you. I promise."

To her surprise Gina didn't argue.

"Promise?"

"I promise!" Chloe tried to make her voice sound strong.

"Can I go to the doctor with you?" Gina desperately wanted to do something.

"I'm going tomorrow at nine AM." Chloe didn't want to tell her that Anita was going, but she knew that Gina would already assume that.

"I'll pick you and Anita up." Gina didn't disappoint.

The front door opened and Savi came bouncing in and jumped in Chloe's lap before she could stop her.

Chloe looked at the chocolate smeared all over her face and attempted a smile.

"Gotta go! The girl is back."

"See you in the morning. Love."

"Love," Chloe said.

Brent stood awkwardly in the kitchen as Chloe found a clean washcloth and wiped off Savi's face.

"I'm going to play, Mommy!" Savi yelled as she ran down the hall toward her bedroom.

Brent and Chloe stood silently staring at one another, the heaviness in the room growing thicker with each second.

"How are you feeling?" he asked quietly.

"Fine." Chloe's voice was clipped as she tried to remember a time when she had loved him. She knew she must have. She remembered it like a distant memory that she had since pushed so far away that it seemed like it was only in her imagination. "We don't have to do this. You're here for Savi and that's it. Thanks for coming back from your trip for her."

"Chlo—" His voice was pleading. "I'm sorry. Can we just talk, please?"

"Thanks for coming back from your work trip but I'm exhausted and need to sleep. Make sure Savi eats something appropriate for dinner." Chloe turned and walked away. As soon as she got out of the room, she allowed the tears to fall that were welling up in her eyes.

I'll never need him again, she told herself. She wrapped her arms tightly around her body trying to hold herself together and keep the pain at bay like she had always done so she wouldn't fall completely apart.

❧ 14 ❧

N eena

NEENA STOOD IN THE MIDDLE OF THE DINING ROOM, FROZEN.

Her chest felt like a giant weight was sitting on it. She couldn't believe she had forgotten that she had all of the money for her school books in her wallet.

She had been planning on going to the bank all week, but it had slipped her mind. She fought back the tears that threatened to spill out.

She had spent hours working for that money, and now it was gone, and she had nobody to blame but herself. School was starting in a week and there was no way she was going to be able to buy her books now.

Her feet felt glued to the floor, unable to move.

A familiar, blonde woman with remarkable blue eyes suddenly appeared next to her. "Are you okay, honey?"

Neena tried to nod but couldn't.

The woman put her arm around her shoulders and even though Neena was several inches taller than her, she collapsed. The woman was strangely strong and guided her to a table where a younger woman who strongly resembled her, sat.

The younger woman pushed a glass of water toward her, urging her to drink.

"Honey, should I call an ambulance or somebody for you? You look like you're about to pass out." The woman who had helped her looked deeply concerned.

Neena shook her head. She was afraid to open her mouth to speak as the women watched her carefully.

"I'm Emerson," the younger woman smiled sympathetically. "Do you need to eat something? How can we help?"

Emerson Grey!

Neena tried not to show her surprise. Of course she was sitting with Emerson and Lillian Grey on the worst day of her life. She'd seen them before around town but had never spoken to them.

"The Grey family is in a different class than we are, baby girl. They don't want to be bothered with us," her daddy had said more than once.

They'd always seemed like ordinary people to her but Neena had noticed how people seemed to be afraid of them in public, even though it didn't make sense.

Neena wanted to throw up. The thought of the drugs her mother could buy with over a thousand dollars made her sick.

"I don't think she's going to pass out, Momma," Emerson said to Lillian. "Maybe we should order her some chicken noodle soup."

"Yes, some of the Cathead's chicken noodle soup will make her feel better," Lillian said decidedly. She stood up and Neena watched her talk to Jennifer Wynn, who was waitressing that day. Lillian looked over and nodded at Neena and Jennifer smiled.

"I don't know if we've ever met." Emerson smiled as she spoke, and Neena was taken by how beautiful and kind Emerson's eyes were as they stared into hers, concerned.

Neena shook her head again, afraid to speak.

"Did you go to school with my boys? Gavin and Garrett?" Emerson prodded gently.

Neena nodded.

The twins had been a year ahead of her and she hadn't known them very well, but everyone knew who they were. The girls loved them though neither boy seemed overly interested in dating. Gavin had been more of the ladies' man, and Garrett focused on school, but that didn't discourage his fan club.

"I thought I recognized you," Emerson smiled again. Neena was taken aback by her gentleness. She had heard stories about the Greys, the oldest and richest family in the harbor, but she had never spoken to them. She knew Emerson's husband had died in a tragic accident a few years prior, and she had felt bad for the boys who had clearly taken it hard.

She knew what it was like to grow up without a parent, and even though they were older, she knew the absence they would feel in their hearts every day after.

Jennifer brought over a piping hot bowl of soup and a Coke and set it down in front of Neena.

"I can't pay for this," Neena blurted it out. "My mom ... she ... stole my purse that had all of my money in it."

Neena tried to hold back the sobs but couldn't any longer as Lillian put her arm around her shoulder.

"It's okay, honey. You don't have to worry about the bill. We'll take care of it." Lillian's voice was soothing as she stroked Neena's hair and comforted her. Neena tried to ignore all of the eyes that were on her in the Cathead, but she knew everyone had to be staring at her being comforted by the Grey's.

It all felt like a bad dream and Neena couldn't stop crying.

When her tears finally dissolved into hiccups, Lillian forced her to drink. "Drink this down, honey. It will make you feel better."

Neena gulped the water down and it was cool against her throat. She felt like she had been crying for hours and finally her hiccups subsided.

"Eat some of Maeve's chicken noodle soup," Emerson said, pushing the bowl toward her. "It'll make anything feel better."

Neena thought about Emerson's dead husband and wondered if Maeve's soup had helped her, too. She picked up her spoon and obediently began to eat the soup. It was delicious and soothing.

"I'm Neena by the way." Neena suddenly felt awkward realizing she had never told them her name. These two women had been so nice to her after she had embarrassed herself in the middle of the restaurant. She knew people would be talking about it for days.

"So, your momma stole your purse?" Emerson asked gently. "Why on earth would she do that?"

Neena knew that Emerson couldn't possibly imagine what it was like to grow up with someone like Vanessa. Lillian must've been the perfect mother and Neena felt a twinge of jealousy.

"She's an addict," Neena stuttered. "I should've known better. I should've taken my money to the bank and put it away like I was supposed to and this never would've happened."

She was angry with herself for being so stupid.

"How much money was in your purse, honey?" Lillian asked.

Neena was ashamed to say. "It was over a thousand dollars. It was for my books, and school starts next week, and I'm never going to be able to earn back the money to buy them by then." Neena started to cry again.

"Oh, honey." Lillian looked up at Emerson and Emerson immediately knew what her momma was going to do.

"Don't you worry about that book money. I'll loan it to you." Lillian whispered in Neena's ear.

"No, ma'am," Neena pushed back in her chair. "I appreciate it, but I can't take your money. I'm not a charity case."

Lillian's eyes were wide, and she looked like she had just been slapped.

"This is not charity." Lillian's voice was steady. "I said it was a loan. You'll pay it back, every cent!"

"Why would you do that? You don't even know me or if I'll repay it." Neena tried not to sound suspicious but she knew that nothing in life came that easily.

"Why wouldn't I?" Lillian countered. "Everyone knows that I have the money and right now, you could use it. Why wouldn't I help you when you're sitting right in front of me? You seem like a perfectly decent young lady who just needs somebody to be kind to her right now." Lillian's blue eyes met Neena's brown ones and they stared at one another for a few long moments.

Finally, Neena broke away.

"How will I pay you back?" Neena whispered feeling defeated.

"What are you good at? What is your gift?" Lillian spoke as though the question was asked of her every day.

Neena was lost. She didn't have any gifts. The only thing she could do well was bake.

Her neighbor, Renee, had taught her how to bake after her mom left the first time. Neena had spent hours in her kitchen taking in the scent of cinnamon, brown sugar, and every spice imaginable. When she wasn't in school or with her daddy she was with Renee.

Renee had been a sweet woman who never married or had children of her own. Neena always felt as though she regretted it because she was so maternal. She wondered about the emptiness Renee must've felt in her soul because she could see it every time she looked at her. Spending time with Renee had made them both forget about the hollowness inside that was left by not having the love they yearned for the most.

When Jaden turned one, Renee had died of a stroke, and every time Neena baked, she thought of her.

"I can bake... really well, actually. I've been told that I'm really good." Neena sounded embarrassed.

"Perfect!" Lillian exclaimed. "I need ten pies for a fundraiser next week. You'll come to my kitchen and make them for me."

"Momma, wouldn't you be able to do more in my kitchen? You don't exactly bake or have the supplies," Emerson reminded her gently.

"Yes, Emerson is right. You'll have to do it at the Grey house. I'm not a baker, and the only thing you'll be able to find to roll crust with is a bottle of vodka," Lillian laughed.

Neena smiled in spite of herself.

This couldn't be happening. Her mom had once again leveled her but somehow it had led her to the Grey's. Neena wanted to pinch herself to see if she was dreaming, but she was afraid that if did she might actually wake up.

15

G ina

"I'VE NEVER SAID THIS TO YOU BEFORE, BUT SOMETIMES YOU CAN BE very mean." Theo was angrier than Gina had ever seen him before.

It was one of numerous arguments they'd been having over the past several weeks since she told him she was pregnant.

Up until then they'd never even argued before. Even when Lincoln and Leo were born, during the time when most couples became disenchanted with one another, they had not. In fact, they had fallen even more in love, but now things were strained between them and even the children took notice.

"Why is Mommy so mad?" Lincoln, the oldest of the two, had asked Theo, his dark eyes full of so much concern for a seven-year-old boy. Even as he colored in his favorite coloring book, he worried over his mom.

"Mommy is just very tired. You have to forgive her. She loves you very much." Theo smoothed down his son's dark curls and kissed him on top of his head.

"Mommy is always mad and tired lately." Lincoln's eyes filled with tears.

Theo had been fielding questions from the boys for weeks and was beyond frustrated. His usually ordered life had been turned upside down by the changes in his beautiful wife. He found that he was short-tempered with everyone but more than that, he felt lost.

They'd been together since their freshman year of college and he had fallen in love with her the moment he saw her. It was the storybook love at first sight romance, and even though she had resisted at first, he was able to win her over.

She was unlike anyone he'd ever met.

Quiet and shy, a steely undercurrent running through her delicate body. She was beautiful in an unassuming way and he couldn't imagine a life without her from the moment she said his name.

There were parts of her that she kept hidden from him.

He always knew that she had a difficult childhood and a brother who had disappeared, but she refused to talk about him or anyone else in her family, and he had accepted her in spite of it. It bothered him that she couldn't share the most painful memories with him.

"I want to share everything about your life with you," he had begged, but she had refused.

"You'll never see me the same ever again, and I couldn't stand to see you look at me differently."

He had met her mother only once as she lay on her deathbed, and it had been awkward and painful as he sat with Gina while she died.

Gina hadn't shed a tear.

Afterwards, Gina had to clean up the mess that her mother had left with the house and all of the medical bills and debts she never had the money to pay. He was never clear about what happened to her dad, but he knew he was dead and assumed it hadn't been a good ending.

Theo had always been patient with Gina because his heart could see that she had suffered more than he could ever imagine.

Though his father was distant and aloof, he had known that his mother had adored him but now his patience was wearing thin. The resentment that he held toward Gina for not wanting their child was more than he'd anticipated. He always thought that if he loved her enough that it would be enough for both of them, and he was faced with the reality that he might be wrong.

He was finding himself sleeping in the guest room more often than he was sleeping in his own bed. He missed how their eyes met every morning and how she kissed him good night in that timid way that made him love her so much.

He had been thrilled at the thought of having another child.

If Gina were willing, he would have ten more. As an only child it had been very lonely. When he imagined his adult life, he could see a house full of children, racing around, making noise.

"I don't want any more than two children, Theo. I can't see how more than that would be manageable or realistic!" Gina's large emerald eyes had pled with him to understand and he pretended like he did. He couldn't resist her.

He thought that once the children were born he would be able to convince her otherwise but she had stuck to the original plan.

"Two. No more." She never even considered having another child.

Theo's parents had both worked and neither was ever home. He'd spent most of his time alone and he didn't want his children to grow up the same. He'd asked if she would consider staying home with the children.

"If I'm not going to work, then my job will be to take care of the house and the children," she had insisted, her long neck rigid and her eyes serious.

"I'll get you as much help as you need. Someone to cook, clean, do the laundry. You won't need to do a thing except take care of the children." He was convinced that she would agree. Who wouldn't? He had women lining up to date him hoping for that kind of life, but she had refused all of it.

He had grown up in a family that never worried about the expense, but she had experienced the opposite.

As he began to notice the tiny bump that protruded from her slender frame, his heart began to explode with happiness just as it had with his first two. He tried to ignore that she didn't feel the same.

"I never realized how mean you can be," Theo repeated.

"I'm not being mean, I'm just trying to get used to the idea of having another baby and I'm having a difficult time! We aren't prepared. We just had the nursery converted to a regular bedroom and now we're going to have to do it all over again." She was frustrated with herself for being so angry, but she couldn't help but blame him for the situation they were in. "Or rather I'm going to have to do it all over again, without your help, just like the other two."

"All you have to do is ask!" Theo threw his hands in the air. "You act like such a martyr, but this is what you wanted. This life of raising babies and running the house."

"Is it? Or is it what *you* wanted? I wanted to be an artist, but you wanted a trophy wife and a stay at home mom to take care of your kids. That's not what I wanted. This wasn't the life I'd ever planned!" Gina's face was red, her neck blotchy, and Theo tried to remember if he had ever seen her so angry.

"I didn't know you felt this way."

"No, you didn't, because you never asked! I've been playing the perfect wife so that you're happy, but have you ever asked if I'm happy? I'm not happy! I didn't realize how unhappy I was until I peed on that stupid stick. "

"But Ginny, we love each other, and we can get through anything." Theo searched her eyes for a glimpse of the girl he fell in love with.

He imagined for a moment that he saw her soften.

"Do you love me? Or do you love the idea of me? You don't even truly know me or what I really want." Gina's voice was hard.

"I know you! At least I know what you allow me to know of you, but you don't let me in. There are plenty of things I want to know but you refuse to let me see you completely. So how much can I know? What should I know?" Theo was frustrated but cautious, Gina's tone foreign to him.

"I don't know if I love you anymore. I don't know how I can love someone who cares so little for me and knows nothing about my feelings."

Theo sucked in his breath, as though someone had punched him in the gut.

"You can't be serious, Ginny." Theo grabbed her wrist and held it tight. "How can you say that you don't know if you love me?"

Gina tore her wrist out of his grasp and Theo realized what he had done. He had never grabbed her before, and the moment of terror in her eyes was enough to scare him, too.

He stared at her face, her face white and her hands trembling.

"Go to work, Theo." Gina shook, her voice hoarse.

"Ginny, honey, I'm so sorry. I didn't mean to..." He tried desperately to apologize but the damage had been done.

"How could you?" Gina fought back the tears, betrayal brimming in her eyes. "Nobody can ever touch me like that, you know this. Why would you even do that?"

"I'm sorry. I'm so sorry." Gina's horrified eyes were reflected in his own. He had only ever touched her out of love.

It had taken him years to build her trust, and the look in her eyes told him it had been shattered by a single touch.

"Please, just go." Gina cried and Theo could see there was no consoling her. He didn't want to leave but he knew that staying would only upset her more.

"We'll talk when I get home, Ginny." Theo's voice was hoarse with sadness. "Again, I'm so sorry. You know I would never hurt you."

Gina refused to look him in the eye as she waited for him to leave.

When she heard the click of the doorknob, she fell to the floor holding herself tightly. It had been many years since she had felt that fear but suddenly, she was six years old again, and her body shook uncontrollably.

She futilely tried to push back the memory of the leather belt as it cut across her skin and the spit that flew against her cheek with each curse. She tried to block out the bruises she had to cover-up when she went to school and the ongoing fear that she would die in her sleep.

As she looked down at her wrist where Theo had grabbed her it came rushing back as though all the years of therapy had never happened.

She sat on the floor in the corner of the kitchen, the smooth linoleum cold against her feet. She rocked as she wrapped her arms tightly around herself and wept uncontrollably.

The terror came to her in a rush, and suddenly Gina knew exactly what she needed to do.

16

A bi

ABI PULLED THE CAR INTO HER PARENT'S DRIVEWAY, HER HEART doing flip-flops.

She cracked her neck and took a deep breath. Riley huffed anxiously.

"I know girl, you have to potty." Abi hooked the leash around her collar and opened her door. Riley obediently followed shaking her long black tail.

Abi cringed, knowing her parents wouldn't love having a dog in the house. Their family dog, Roxie, had died when Abi was fifteen, and her dad had vowed he would never get another. Abi was convinced that he had loved that dog more than his own children, so when Roxie died, he was inconsolable.

Abi was sure he would love Riley but knew that she would have to suffer the consequences of bringing her unannounced first.

Dominic and Lexi bounded out of the car.

Lexi pointed at Riley. "Why she gotta poop in the front yard?"

Dominic laughed. "That's where dogs poop, duh! Where do you think they're gonna poop? In the bathroom?"

Lexi fell into a fit of giggles.

The front door opened and Anita came out. Abi knew immediately that something was off. Anita's usually perfect make up was smeared, and she looked like she had just woken up from a nap. She had never known her mother to leave the house with anything less than perfect hair or make up.

"Is everything all right, Mom?" Abi asked.

"Dominic! Lexi? Come give Nonny a hug!" Anita ignored her.

Both children obediently ran into her waiting arms and hugged her. Riley barked with excitement as Abi try to calm her down.

"Mom, are you okay?" Abi repeated.

"Do I look like I'm okay?" Anita snapped.

"No, Mom. That's why I'm asking." Abi already regretted coming home.

"I'm sorry. I know you just got here, but the last twenty-four hours have been crazy."

"Are you going to tell me what is going on?" Abi tried to be patient but getting Anita to tell her anything was a struggle as it had been all her life.

"Chloe is sick, Sissy. She has a tumor, and I don't know how bad it is, and her stupid idiot husband Brent has been cheating on her with a girl in his office. I just don't know what's going to happen." Anita's usually tanned face looked grey and withered.

Abi felt as though she had been slapped in the face, her head suddenly spinning. She had never liked Brent; always worried that something like this would happen. His flirtatious and easy-going manner seemed to mask something darker, and she realized that she always knew he was capable of hurting her sister.

She thought guiltily about how she hadn't talked to Chloe for months.

"Where is Chloe now?" Abi asked, half expecting her mom to tell her she was inside. She knew how manipulative Anita could be, especially in a situation like this.

"She's at her house with Brent and Savi," Anita sniffed. "I told her she could stay with us, but she refused. She wanted Savi to have some normalcy, and apparently being with her Nonny and Papaw wasn't going to provide that."

Abi was surprised that Chloe had let Brent stay. Usually so decisive, Chloe didn't take shit from anyone. Once her mind was made up there was no changing it. This was a strange act from her sister. Even when Abi found out Todd was cheating on her, she had thrown him out immediately. It had surprised her that she had that much strength. She had never known how much she was capable of until then.

She held back tears. Her heart was heavy for Chloe who had always carried everything so well.

"How bad, Mom?" Abi felt like she had been punched in the gut.

"We don't know yet. You got here at a good time. Chloe is going to need you."

Abi sucked in her breath. She watched as the kids played on the front lawn with Riley. She tried to ignore that her mom hadn't even hugged her yet as she considered the weight that had just been dropped at her shoulders. She knew what it meant.

Any hope of her leaving Grey's Harbor was gone. Obliterated with the news of Chloe's cancer. If she had been honest, she would've admitted it to herself before they left and tried to pack more in, but she was pretending that she might go back, but not now.

"Clearly, Chloe and I do not know how to pick our men," Abi said, more to herself.

"Yes! You would think the two of you would have chosen better. Like I did." Anita said pointedly. "I don't know how both of you would marry such unfaithful men. Then again, I'm sure you weren't easy to live with."

Abi bit her tongue.

She sighed as she turned and began to unpack the car. She watched as Anita ushered the kids in the house. Without a word she grabbed Riley's leash and took her inside.

Abi fought the urge to smoke. It had been four months, two weeks, and four days since she'd smoked a cigarette. It had been even longer since she'd had sex. She hated having vices and wanted to have better self-control for her and the kids who had begged her to quit smoking.

"It smells, Mommy," Lexi had complained, and Dominic agreed.

She'd started smoking with Todd when they first started dating and had quit when she was pregnant with both kids but had gone back to it. Smoking cleared her mind, but she knew she needed to quit so she did, cold turkey. She was happy she did, especially now since cancer was a clear and present danger.

Still, the urge to light up nagged at her and she fought hard against the urge to get in the car and buy a pack or two or three.

She looked at the house and forced herself to walk toward it. She had grown up here, in Grey's Harbor and in this house, but she'd run away as fast as she could, eager to escape the unbearable control that Anita tried to have over her.

Moving away had given her independence and confidence. As she stood in the middle of the sidewalk she felt herself begin to wither into the girl she had once been, so compliant and unable to stand up for herself against parents who never saw her for who she was.

This was going to be so much harder than she'd imagined. With Chloe sick, she wondered what that meant for her, not because Chloe would need her but because Anita would suffocate her with her neediness.

She'd hoped for a fresh start in Grey's Harbor and a chance to possibly even find love again. But as dread began to creep through her, she doubted she would ever get the chance to find either.

❧ 17 ❧

C hloe

CHLOE SIPPED HER TEA AND RUBBED HER TEMPLES, ALTHOUGH IT never helped.

Gina had made her feel better, like she usually did, but as always she reminded her of Linc.

She had spent years pushing Linc out of her mind and she no longer constantly wondered where he was in the world or even *if* he still existed. Even though he had done the unforgivable, she still felt as though a piece of her was wherever he was.

She sighed.

She thought for a split second that maybe that was the reason Brent had cheated on her. Deep down he might've sensed that Chloe had always reserved the biggest part of her heart for Linc, hoping he might return. She shook her head at the thought causing it to pulse even harder.

No! There was no excuse for what he had done.

Who he had done.

Her thoughts drifted back to Linc, and she smiled a sad smile. She pictured his bright green eyes, so much like his sister's. She had spent hours staring into them, promising that when they were older that life would get better.

She had dreamt about them, and when they looked at her, they warmed her in places she never knew existed until she met him. His eyes could see directly into her soul, and she knew she would be looking into them for the rest of her life.

Then one day he was gone. Gina's mom said he ran away but Chloe couldn't believe that he would leave them without a single word. There were no good-byes and no notes.

He just vanished.

The police tagged him as a runaway, but as time went on, Chloe never doubted that he would leave her. Gina was like a ghost, unable to talk about the night he disappeared, and Chloe held onto that as a sign. She knew Gina was fragile, and shortly after she left to live with her aunt and uncle in Gilmore, but they remained bonded in their despair.

Chloe tried to ignore the ache in her heart every time she thought of him. It had been so long since she had kissed his lips or her heard him whisper her name.

She had met Brent in college, and even though he wasn't Linc, he awakened a part of her heart that was still beating.

She had missed Linc during every important moment of her life always wishing he was there with her, especially now. She knew he would make her feel better and safe and she needed that more than she needed the air she breathed.

The last time she had seen him was an ordinary day. They had skipped school and doubled back to her house so they could spend time together. As they lie in her bed, her parents gone for the day, their naked limbs entwined, she knew she could never be happier than any time of her life. She had traced her fingers over his chest lingering on the deep scar.

He flinched.

She knew he was sensitive, but she knew everything about him.

"You don't have to hide from me," Chloe had said kissing the scar. "I love everything about you, especially this scar."

"You don't know everything, Chlo," Linc's voice was husky, as he whispered into her ear. His lips made her hips clinch as she tightened her legs around his naked hips.

"I do know everything, just like you know everything about me. We are meant to be, you and me. We're the same."

In one sudden movement he flipped her on her back, her heart racing. She looked up at him and marveled at his strong jaw line and perfect face. She had been watching him grow into this beautiful man and was amazed that he would ever love her.

"You don't wanna love me, Chlo. There are things you don't know that I'll never tell you. I don't know why you've made me fall in love with you the way you have but this isn't good for either of us. We're just going to end up hurting one another in the end. Nothing good ever happens to people in my family." He ran his tongue over her stomach and up to her breasts, expertly circling each nipple. In one sudden movement he was inside of her and she gasped in surprise and pleasure.

It had always been this way with them, like two magnets drawn to one another as though they had no control. Even before she knew she loved him, she wanted him with a desire she'd never even known she could possess.

As he drove inside of her as he had so many times before, she let her mind go deliciously blank, her hips thrusting against him in the beautiful dance they had perfected.

He exploded without warning, her body going numb as she reached hers, too, her cries reverberating throughout the empty house.

He lay on top of her panting, his lips still warm and wanting as he kissed her ferociously.

"I don't wanna love you like I do, and I wish I didn't. But God, you're the best thing that's ever happened in my life, and I don't want to ever lose you. I don't deserve you. I swear I don't."

"Stop, Linc. We deserve to be happy and loved. With the shit parents we have and the fucked up lives we're trying to get out of, we deserve this. I'm going to make you happy for as long as you'll let me." Chloe hated when he talked like that.

They were the only thing good and right in each other's lives, and when he doubted their love, it took days to get it back on track. He was getting better, but his parents never gave him much to believe in.

"I want to believe you. I do." He laid his head on her shoulder, and they stayed frozen in the moment for what seemed like hours.

He looked at his watch and rolled off of her, kissing her hard before he started getting dressed. Chloe hadn't thought much of it at the time, but he had been telling her goodbye.

Chloe wished a thousand times a day that she could go back in time and relive that moment with him. She could never imagine loving anyone even half as much.

As many times as Chloe had tried to get Gina to talk about it, she had refused, unable to share with her best friend the events of that night. Chloe knew that it was all connected to Linc's disappearance but there was nothing she could do. Everyone who knew the answer was either gone or unable or to talk about it.

Including her love, Lincoln.

Chloe held on to the moments she was always afraid she would lose. She closed her eyes and pictured his smile and the way his voice sounded in her ear. She thought about their first kiss hidden in her backyard shed, and the first time they lay naked with one another, neither of them sure of what to do.

He had been everything to her, but he had been gone for ten years, and she was angry with him for leaving her, especially now when she needed him the most, when she needed him to make her feel safe.

I don't want to die, she whispered to herself.

She imagined what he would say if he were with her.

It would be the same thing he said the night when he first met her all of those years ago at midnight in their back yard. He'd been swinging on their swing set, undetected until she'd exploded out of the house, her hair flying in every direction.

He'd waited until her sobbing was down to a messy hiccup. She told him the entire story of how she had finished washing every dish in the cabinets because she hadn't done a good job washing dishes, which was her daily chore.

"Are you trying to kill us?" Her mother had waved a dirty fork in front of her face. "You'll rewash every plate, cup, and piece of silverware in this house until you learn to do things the right way the first time."

She was exhausted but she didn't want to cry in front of Abi, so she ran outside when she was done to get fresh air.

"It'll be okay, kid. Whatever you have going on can't be as bad as the shitty thing going on in my house right now." A cigarette hung out of his mouth and Chloe thought that she'd never seen anyone so beautiful in her entire life.

"Who are you and why are you in my yard?" Chloe's eyes were wide.

"I'm Linc, your new neighbor. I'm sorry. We just moved here, and I have nowhere to go, and I definitely do not want to stay inside." He turned to leave but it was the last thing Chloe wanted.

"Wait!" She called out, reaching for his cigarette. "I know somewhere we can go."

❦ 18 ❧

eena

NEENA STOOD ON THE MASSIVE PORCH, HER KNEES TREMBLING. Never in a million years had she ever imagined that she would end up standing on Emerson Grey's porch.

This was the day she was supposed to bake pies in Emerson's kitchen. She was excited and terrified.

She took a deep breath, her heart skipping as she heard footsteps approaching the door.

"Neena!" Emerson's warm voice floated through the door. Neena heard her before she saw her and when she finally appeared, Neena couldn't help but smile back. Emerson's wide smile was contagious.

"Hi, Emerson." Neena suddenly felt shy.

"Please, come in. We have everything you need. Are you hungry? We should eat before you get started."

"No, I'm fine." Just then Neena's stomach grumbled, betraying her, and she realized with embarrassment that she had forgotten to each lunch.

"I'm making a sandwich. You'll have one." It was a statement, not a question.

"I-I-I don't want to put you out..." Neena stuttered. She was usually the one making the sandwiches. Her dad was a terrible cook and she had often wondered how he had managed to keep her alive. She learned at an early age that she had a knack for anything that involved cooking and baking so she always did.

"It's no trouble. I was making myself one anyway. Don't be shy. Make yourself at home."

Neena was far from comfortable. As she stepped into the home, it took her breath away.

As the light shone through the large stained-glass windows in the front foyer, the sounds and salty smell of the ocean resonated through the home. The view of the water as it lapped against the beach was stunning, and Neena thought she had never seen anything so beautiful.

It was bright and welcoming and Neena never wanted to leave. Neena realized that she had never imagined what it would be like in the house of a Grey.

Emerson saw her staring at the windows and smiled. "Do you like the stained glass?"

"Oh... yes, it's beautiful!" Neena sighed. "I've never seen anything like them before."

"We just had them put in recently. Have you met Maddy Grey? We've recently connected with her in the past couple of years. Even though she's a Grey, we didn't know her for a while, but we're so happy to have her in the family. She's a very talented artist and we commissioned her to do these for us."

"I haven't met her, but she does marvelous work." Neena admired the intricate design and the way the bright colors danced on the walls, sparkling with the sunshine.

She pulled herself away from the windows and followed Emerson into the kitchen.

Even though the Grey family was well known throughout the Harbor, until the day at the Cathead Diner, she had never met any one of them before. She knew that Jaxx Stockman and Maddy Grey had just gotten married, but she had only seen them around town a few times.

The Grey legacy was a long and complicated one, and there were many stories about them, but Neena had been surprised to realize that Emerson and Lillian were just kind and normal people.

Even though they weren't.

They had more money than Neena would ever see in her entire life but sitting in Emerson's kitchen, she watched her make sandwiches, and she wondered if Emerson even cared about any of it.

"Can I ask you a personal question?" Emerson's voice cut through Neena's thoughts, startling her.

"Oh... sure." Neena tried to imagine what Emerson would want to know about her.

Emerson's voice shook slightly as she stared hard at the sandwich she was putting together. "I just... I wondered if you ever missed your mom. I mean... I don't know the circumstances and it's really personal, but I just wondered. If you don't mind."

Neena's eyes immediately filled up with tears.

"Oh God, I didn't mean to make you cry, I'm so sorry! Forget I even said anything. God... I'm sorry... I knew I shouldn't ask, but it's been bothering me ever since that day at the Cathead. I wondered what kind of mother would steal from her own child. But even as upset as you were, you seemed disappointed, but not angry. I... I shouldn't have asked. I overstepped..."

"No! Don't be sorry!" Neena sniffed. "I'm not crying because you hurt my feelings. It's just that... nobody has ever asked me if I missed my mom before. Not even my dad."

Emerson put down the knife she was using to cut the sandwiches and wiped her hands on her pants before she walked around to hug Neena.

"Oh... I just thought it would be a natural question. I grew up without a father and I wondered if you ever missed her. My sons lost their father a couple of years ago and... I know they miss him, but they never say. They won't talk about it."

Neena smiled through her tears.

"I think that everyone expects me to be so strong. My mom... she's been an addict for so long that it's just the way it is. Nobody ever asked me how I felt about it before."

"You don't have to tell me. I was being too personal. I'm sorry."

"No... Thank you for asking. The truth is... I do miss her. I mean... I don't actually miss *her*. She was never around the way most moms are and when she was, I was always waiting for her to leave because that's what she did. My dad raised me ever since I was a baby. I miss the thought of her... of what she should've been or what she could've been."

Emerson nodded as she set a thick roast beef sandwich in front of Neena and a large iced tea, then settled in with her lunch at the counter opposite of her.

"My mom raised me by herself. She was strong and I never missed having a father. I had a surrogate father for a time, John, but then he died and I barely remembered him. I guess... I never missed having a father until I married Sawyer and we had children of our own. He was such a good dad, and it made me wonder what it would've been like. It's strange how you can miss someone you never knew." Emerson took a small bite of her sandwich.

"H-h-how have you been since you've lost your husband?" The conversation had taken a deep and personal tone and Neena screwed up the courage to ask before she lost her nerve.

Emerson's eyes welled up and Neena instantly regretted that she'd asked.

"I'm sorry..."

"No, please don't be sorry! It's just... nobody asks me how I'm doing anymore. They assume that I'm okay now that..." Emerson looked thoughtfully at the sparkling diamond ring on her left ring finger.

"You're engaged?" Neena admired how her ring sparkled in the sunlight that shone through the kitchen skylight.

"Yes, I love Ethan more than I ever imagined I could, but I'll never stop loving Sawyer. He was my first love and the father of my children. Thank you for asking."

They ate in silence, both lost in memories of love that had been lost.

"Wow... we covered a lot of ground in a short time," Emerson broke the comfortable silence.

"Yes, we did." Neena smiled.

"You know, I like you, Neena. I'm so happy we met at the Cathead. It's like Mom and I were meant to be there that day. I can't explain it but I feel like we were destined to be friends."

Neena blushed. She'd never had anyone who was so happy to meet her before and she wondered if the warmth from Emerson was anything like the love of a mother.

"Well, now that I've talked your ear off and made you feel completely awkward, I suppose I should let you get to work on the pies."

Neena took a last long drink of her tea and moved over to the sink to wash her hands.

"Thank you for the sandwich. It was delicious." She was usually the one making the sandwiches and having someone take care of her felt nice.

"Anytime. You'll have to visit again, on a day when I'm not putting you to work." Emerson laughed. Neena marveled at how easily she laughed. She glowed in the warmth of her new friendship as she set to work.

"Wow... you thought of everything!" Neena looked around.

Emerson clearly knew her way around the kitchen and had prepared everything Neena would need.

"Let me know if I missed anything," Emerson smiled at the expression on Neena's face.

Just then the kitchen door opened and Neena sucked in her breath. Gavin Grey entered the room, shirtless and sweaty, panting from a run on the beach.

"Hello, sweetheart," Emerson beamed as she offered her cheek up for a kiss.

"Hi, Mom." Gavin obliged, smiling at Neena. "Who's your friend?"

"This is Neena. I met her at the Cathead last week and she's going to make some pies for our fundraiser."

"Cool." Gavin's eyes lit up at the mention of pie. "Any chance there might be an extra apple pie for me?"

Neena felt her cheeks warm. "Um... I'm sure I can make an extra."
She felt like she couldn't breathe.

Gavin was as good looking up close as he was from far away and had only gotten more handsome as he grew older. She had never talked to him in school because she was too shy and doubted he remembered her.

"Mrs. Klein, junior year, you sat in the third seat from the front." He stared deep into her dark brown eyes as though he was reading her mind.

Neena started. "Yes, that was me!"

"That's what I thought. I never forget a pretty face." Gavin winked at her and walked out of the room, leaving Neena's mouth hanging open.

She looked at Emerson who gave her a sly smile.

Suddenly, she realized that she hadn't been invited over just to make pies.

❧ 19 ❧

G ina

THEO WAS PANICKED AT THE THOUGHT OF LOSING GINA.

The look of terror in her eyes stayed with him all morning as the guilt ate away at him. He could never hurt her. It wasn't in his DNA, yet he had grabbed at her wrist in frustration.

He had never even raised his voice at her, and when most husbands might've gotten angry, he didn't. He knew that he was wired differently than most men he knew, but he was content. He knew who he was and that he loved Gina more than anyone he could ever imagine, except his own mother.

They'd never even had a fight.

After everything that she'd been through he couldn't imagine anything trivial coming between them.

It had taken a long time for her to trust him but when she did, she had broken his heart with stories of her childhood, even allowing him to see the scars that were left behind. Theo knew that if her parents weren't already dead that he would've wanted to kill them.

He imagined the mini version of Gina and vowed from the moment he knew he loved her that he would always protect her, and he'd kept his promise.

Until now.

When she shriveled as he grabbed her, he felt something between them break and he was desperate to fix it.

He'd always been able to fix things.

It was what he did. He could smooth over and make anything right, but he wasn't sure if he could do it with this. She had looked at him like he was a monster and he wasn't sure if he could ever forgive himself or gain her trust again.

He had worked through lunch unable to eat, in agony over it all day.

He jumped when his phone beeped. Gina's face lit up in his phone and he leapt out of his chair.

"Chloe has cancer." Her voice was small and broken and his heart immediately ached.

"What?" Theo's mouth went dry.

Chloe and Gina had spent more than half their lives together and were closer than sisters. Theo knew how much pain Gina was in. "I'll be right there."

She hadn't asked but he knew that she needed him.

There was no question in his mind that he needed to be with her at the moment.

His mind was swirling.

Chloe.

Cancer.

But Gina had called.

She had needed him and she had called.

Even though he had scared her, she wasn't done with him, and as he drove as fast as he could to get to her, all he could think about was that he needed to hold her.

Chloe.

He couldn't imagine their lives without Chloe, and he had a million questions running through his mind.

Cancer.

He fucking hated cancer. It had taken his beautiful mother and he hated it.

"Tell me what you need."

"I need Chloe to not have cancer," Gina cried.

"How bad, honey?"

"Bad? I don't know how good or bad, but it's in her brain so there's no chance of any of it being good." The exasperation and frustration in Gina's voice was growing. Theo knew that before long she'd be hysterical and he needed to get to her before it got to that both for her sake and the life growing inside of her.

"Where are you, honey?" Theo asked.

"I'm home." Gina's voice was barely audible.

"I'm on the way." Theo said as he grabbed his jacket off of the chair in his office. He yelled to his secretary to move all of his appointments as he rushed out the door.

"You didn't have to leave work," Gina moaned miserably. "I don't even know what's happening right now. I don't even know why I called. Especially when..."

Theo didn't let her finish her sentence. "You called because I'm your best friend and you need me. I'm sorry for what happened, and I would take it back in a second if I could. I would never hurt you."

She had called and that told Theo that she'd forgiven him even if she wasn't ready to admit it yet.

He should've had more faith in her. He had to have known it would take more than that to shake her. She and her brother, Linc, had experienced awful things with their parents.

They were horrors that seemed completely out place in a beautiful seaside town like Grey's Harbor.

He had never imagined that things like that happened to people here. He had grown up with the beautiful sandy beaches and the bright blue sky, never imagining there was a darker, uglier side to the place he loved so much.

For a time, he had considered moving but she had refused. As much as she hated her past, she loved Grey's Harbor. She was addicted to the donuts at Anna's bakery and the coffee from Shifting Dunes.

She always claimed there was no better pizza than her favorite veggie pizza at Harbor New York.

She had grown up in the harbor and had never wanted to leave. But Theo knew that she also didn't want to leave in case Linc might return.

Theo had secretly invested thousands of dollars and employed numerous private detectives to try and find him, with no luck. Gina often cried out his name in her dreams, and Theo knew she missed him more than she would admit.

He wanted to find him for her.

He understood loss. He had felt it when his mother had passed, leaving him alone. Without Gina, he wouldn't have had anyone.

He had been naive of other people's suffering until he met her. She opened his eyes to the reality of the world around him and other people's misery. It changed his heart in ways he could never explain to anyone else.

She hadn't even trusted him with any of it until they had been dating for nearly a year, making sense of the distance she kept between them, even when they were together.

She finally told him about the abuse in between sobs and hushed tones, whispering it to him as though if she raised her voice, she might completely relive it again.

She told him everything after he had told her he loved her for the first time.

Even if it meant he would never look at her the same.

Much to her surprise, he considered her even more beautiful for being so strong yet enduring so much.

He raced to get home to her, his chest heavy. He knew how miserable she would be at even the slightest possibility of losing Chloe. They had suffered so much together. He was driving too fast, and as he passed the place where Maeve Wynn had her accident a few years before, the sun glare caught him off guard. As he tried to block the bright light from his eyes, he heard a horn blaring as he blindly searched to find the direction it was coming from.

The sound of tires squealing made his heart pound in his chest as he desperately tried to steer his truck out of danger.

All he could think about was Gina and the kids as he skidded out of control, sweat pouring from his brow.

Gina!

He thought about her beautiful face and his children's as he closed his eyes and prayed.

I'm so sorry, Gina. I'm so sorry!

20

A^{bi}

"GRAB THE KIDS, ABI!" ANITA'S VOICE BROKE THROUGH ABI'S thoughts as she unpacked, placing her clothes neatly in the dresser drawers of her old bedroom.

The kids were settling into Chloe's old room, not wanting to separate from one another even though there was plenty of room in the house for each to have their own bedroom.

They were used to sharing a room in the apartment, and even though Anita thought it was silly for them to stay together, she had other things on her mind that were more important.

"Abi, lets go!" Anita pushed open the door without knocking.

Abi took a deep breath, raking her fingers through her hair.

"We're going to get Chloe some groceries and drop them at the house. Lord only knows what she's been feeding Savi or whether her useless cheating husband will even help. You may have to stay there with her a few nights a week." Anita barked at Abi and Abi was suddenly reduced to the pawn she had once been.

Her mother reminded her of why she moved so far away even though she actually loved the harbor and had been desperately homesick for the first year she was gone. She had grown up walking her favorite beach alone, her toes in the soft sand, and she could think of nothing better.

Then she married Todd and had the opportunity to move hours away where Anita no longer had power over her, and she leapt at the chance. Anita had never seen her for who she was. To her, she was simply a person to order around, and she had forgotten how the sound of Anita's voice made her cringe like nails on a chalkboard.

"I'd like to clean up and unpack. Can you give me a little time?" Abi tried not to sound impatient, but she was tired from the long drive and barely had time to stretch her legs or catch her breath.

"You would think you would want to see your sister as soon as possible," Anita huffed.

Anita's voice trailed off as she yelled for the kids. Riley was barking and she could hear her dad yelling for him to stop. She had forgotten how chaotic life in the Caldwell house had always been and she already longed for the peace and quiet of her apartment.

She rubbed her forehead and took a deep breath. She hadn't even been able to think or process that her big sister had cancer. She couldn't imagine a world without her, even though she wasn't surprised that Brent had cheated on Chloe, the way Todd cheated on her. It hurt her heart that they hadn't been able to share their pain with each other, but Anita had never encouraged them to be close, pushing them apart because it was easier for her to manipulate them that way. Divide and conquer.

As Abi wandered down the steps, she stared at the pictures that still hung in the hallway of her and Chloe.

The photo of her, Chloe, and her parents posed casually and happily in matching white shirts on the beach gave her an ugly feeling down in her core. Her mom had been screaming at them the entire ride about how ungrateful they were because they were ten minutes behind schedule. The words "lazy, ungrateful bitches" echoed in Abi's memory as she stared at the beautiful blue sky, the soft sandy beach, and the smiling family of strangers that gave nothing unpleasant away.

Abi had nearly hyperventilated before the photo shoot, her anxiety at an all-time high, and Chloe had to squeeze her hand to try and calm her down like she usually did.

The picture of her parents kissing on their wedding day didn't reveal how they now slept in separate bedrooms, and the picture of Chloe in her cheerleading outfit didn't reflect the eating disorder she battled from middle school up through high school. It was an illness that was rooted in Anita's insistence that Chloe was too thick around the middle and one she still struggled with in spite of everyone's insistence that she needed to put on a few pounds.

Abi hated how the pictures lied.

Even as she grew older, she hated being in pictures unless it was with the kids. That was the only time Abi ever felt like her true self. Being home made her worry that her life with them would be over and that Anita would control every aspect of life as she knew it, just as she had before.

Chloe had married Brent as quickly as she could, right out of high school so that she could get out of the house. Abi had thought it was a mistake, but Chloe had insisted that she loved him even though Chloe knew otherwise.

She had held her sister every night for weeks after Linc had disappeared and knew she couldn't possibly love anyone else as much as she had loved him.

Abi was sure he would return, but Chloe cried as though he were gone forever. "He's never coming back, Abs. He's gone. He would never leave me this way. He's never coming back to me, I know it."

Abi had always known that the Cooke family house was dysfunctional, but she didn't know why Linc would leave so abruptly. She had never trusted him, but Chloe was in love. Not too long after he left, she met Brent and within two months of high school graduation, they had moved in together and were married within six.

He had always made Abi uncomfortable, and a few years later when a drunken Brent asked her to unbutton her shirt and show him her tits because her uptight sister never would, Abi knew their marriage was doomed. But by then, she'd had problems of her own, already suspecting that Todd wasn't being faithful, and she had put Chloe's doomed marriage on the back burner.

She always regretted not telling Chloe about Brent and thought that if she had told her, it might have saved her from the heartache, but Abi had been too self-absorbed at the time and the guilt had kept her from Chloe.

She wondered if Chloe would even want to see her. The last time they had talked, Chloe had been angry with her.

"You're not a kid anymore, Abs. You need to get a real job. Waitressing isn't going to cut it forever." Abi hated when Chloe used her mom voice.

"I make good money, and it's flexible! Todd's been having a hard time finding work and waitressing is a reliable form of income for us." Abi was frustrated that Todd had been away so much but wasn't bringing in any money. His explanations for his absences were wearing thin and she was beginning to suspect that something wasn't right.

"I told you that if you come home, I can get you an entry level job in the firm and you'll get paid well. Better than what you're making now."

"I... don't want to come home right now. I'm not ready to come home." Abi couldn't believe she was having this conversation with Chloe. She always thought Chloe understood why she needed to stay away.

"If it's because you don't want to deal with Mom and Dad, you need to get over it. You're an adult now. You just have to push back." Chloe huffed. Abi was jealous that Chloe had learned to deal with her parents but she hadn't.

"I don't ... I just can't, Chloe. I'm not you. You're stronger than I am. Mom doesn't... she doesn't listen to me... she ... doesn't care about how I feel. Besides, you can do no wrong, you know that? You're different than me."

"She doesn't care how I feel either. I just stopped giving a shit a long time ago, Abs. "

"I'm... just not like you. I wish I was, but I just ... can't." Abi's anxiety started creeping up the moment Chloe began talking to her about moving back home.

As she looked around her bedroom, Abi recalled that conversation like it had been yesterday, even though it had already been over a year before. She hadn't talked to Chloe much after that, a chasm growing between them that seemed nearly impossible to cross.

She knew Chloe was disappointed.

She was always disappointed where Abi was concerned but it was easier to ignore when she was hundreds of miles away, hidden in her tiny apartment where nothing else existed.

But it mattered now.

"Abigail, let's go! Your sister is waiting for us!"

Abi's stomach churned.

She took a deep breath and pushed down her anxiousness, willing her hands to stop trembling.

"I'm coming, Chloe," she whispered under her breath. "I just hope you'll be happy to see me."

21

C hloe

CHLOE THOUGHT BACK TO THAT FIRST NIGHT SHE HAD MET LINC. She'd never smoked until that night, or since. She had eventually convinced Linc to quit too, the smell of it nauseating to her.

That first night she wasn't sure about him until they started walking, her short legs pumping hard to stay in stride with his long ones. As they began walking around the neighborhood, Chloe knew that her dad would eventually come looking for her. At thirteen, her parents were overly protective about everything but walking with him seemed like the most important thing she could be doing at the moment.

He was running from something and she was, too.

"What shitty thing is happening in your house?" Chloe asked, slightly afraid of the answer this boy she had just met would give her.

"I could tell you, but you wouldn't believe it anyway. Let's just say that my parents are total shit bags." Linc's eyes were dark and Chloe thought she could see green in them as he described the people who he should love the most.

"I'm not a fan of my parents either right now," Chloe complained.

"Why? Did Mommy and Daddy take away your allowance?"

Chloe knew he was making fun of her, and she felt her face get warm. "No! That was rude."

"Feisty!" He smiled, completely disarming her. She hadn't expected how his face transformed with a simple change in expression.

"Sorry." She immediately felt bad for overreacting.

"Don't be sorry. I was being a dick. I deserved it."

Chloe nodded.

"So... where did you come from?" Chloe asked, suddenly curious about the boy that materialized in her backyard.

"We're from everywhere," Linc looked around him, taking in the harbor. "We've moved around a lot. My parents don't like to stay in one place for very long."

"I've lived in Grey's Harbor my entire life," Chloe volunteered the information. "I love it here even if I don't like my parents."

"I guess it would be weird if you did," Linc's voice was low. "I don't know anyone who likes their parents."

Chloe was getting nervous. They had been walking a while and she knew her parents would be wondering where she was.

"Should we stop and go back?" It was as though Linc had read her mind.

"Let's keep walking a little longer." Chloe knew she was risking a lot. Her parents would be wondering where she was, but she didn't want to pull herself away from this boy.

"Have you ever been here before?" Chloe asked.

"No. I don't know why my parents decided to settle here. They're renting and this is the nicest neighborhood we've ever lived in. I don't know how they can afford it," Linc admitted, immediately embarrassed, his face flushing red.

"Do you have any brothers or sisters?" The more he talked, the more curious she became.

"I have a sister. She's probably close to your age... "

Chloe's eyes lit up.

Abi was only seven and with as strict as her parents were, Chloe was lonely much of the time.

"She's not... friendly," Linc cautioned.

"Oh..." Chloe tried not to let him see how disappointed she was.

"I mean. ... She's nice. She's a great kid, she's just... quiet."

Chloe could tell he was holding something back.

"We should turn around." Chloe felt a tug in her chest. She knew she was going to be in trouble, and the longer she stayed away the more she would get in.

"Chloe!"

She whipped her head around at the sound of her name.

"Get your ass in the car right now, young lady."

Her dad was driving slowly behind them, his window down as he yelled.

His face was twisted angrily as he glared at her, then at Linc.

"Right fucking now!"

Chloe trembled.

"Tell him to fuck off," Linc whispered angrily under his breath.

"No. Uh... I'm sorry." Chloe raced toward the waiting car, not even sure if he heard her.

Her heart was pounding. She had barely closed the door when the car took off, tires squealing.

"Who in the hell was that and what were you two doing? Where were you going with him?" Spit flew out of his mouth as he yelled at her.

"He's... just a boy. The new neighbor boy."

"The neighbor boy? Who told you that you could leave the house? Where were you going?"

The way he asked made her squirm.

"We were just walking, Dad."

"There's only one reason why you'd be walking with a boy in the dark. One reason."

"Stop... no. We were just taking a walk, I swear."

"You're too young to be a slut. You better keep your legs closed and stay away from that boy. He looked like a piece of shit and I don't want you anywhere near him. You're grounded for two weeks! You're lucky that's all you're getting."

Chloe shuddered as she thought about the sting of the belt on her backside. She was surprised her punishment was so lenient.

When they arrived home she ran to her room and closed the door.

Chloe recalled spending a lot of time in her room, and it wasn't the first time she would ever get in trouble for spending time with Linc.

As the next couple of years went by, she spent as much time with him and Gina as she could. He had been wrong about Gina. Even though she was quiet, she took to Chloe, their bond immediate and strong.

Chloe could never explain it but she recognized something in Gina that was a reflection of herself.

Pain.

Loneliness.

Sadness.

Fear.

Jolted back to the present, Chloe realized she was still the same girl she was then. Her dad no longer called her names and her mom kept her hands to herself, no longer reaching out lightning quick to slap her in the face, but Chloe was still afraid every day. She had spent a lifetime hiding it from the world, but the fear still lived deep down inside of her trying to push its way out.

Now a new fear had arrived, and Chloe doubted she could hide from it.

The tumor terrified her.

Not because she was afraid to die, but because she knew that if she did, she would leave Gina behind, and Savi would remember her as the mother she never wanted to be.

"Shit." She laid her head in her hands and sighed.

Her phone beeped.

She opened the text.

We're on the way over with Abi and her kids. We have groceries.

Her mom never asked. She just showed up. She didn't care if Chloe wanted her there or not.

"Shit," she repeated.

She closed her eyes and thought about that first night with Linc. That first walk, their first kiss, and she cried knowing she would never see him again.

22

Neena

Neena had spent hours baking, and by the time she was finished, she was exhausted.

"These pies look and smell amazing, Neena," Gavin sniffed close to one of the apple pies and Neena smiled.

"That one is for you," she said, washing her hands vigorously in the sink.

"For me?" Gavin's eyes were wide, a smile spreading across his chiseled features. "I don't believe anyone except my momma has ever made me a pie before."

Neena blushed and turned away.

"I bet you're hungry." Gavin looked at her hopefully.

"I really should get home... Daddy and Jaden haven't eaten yet and... "

"Oh, I see. You always make dinner? What if we sent them a pizza and an antipasto salad from Harbor New York and then you and I can grab some of Maeve's meatloaf? What do you think about that?"

He pulled out his phone and asked her for her address. Within minutes, he tapped his phone.

"Done," he gave her a big smile, his teeth perfectly straight and white. "Your family will receive their food in thirty minutes."

"Oh, thank you," she murmured, her cheeks warm.

Neena had never met anyone like Gavin before.

He was understated in his soft grey tee-shirt and broken in blue jeans that hung just right on his waist. He was quiet but confident, which caught her off guard. Most of the guys she knew were obnoxious and her dating experience had been limited because she hadn't met anyone who could hold her attention.

Why would Gavin Grey want to spend time with her?

"I thought it would be a good way to get to know each other. Make new friends." Gavin smiled as though reading her mind. He reached out and gently swiped at her cheek with his thumb. "Flour."

"Oh, thank you!" she managed to croak out, blushing again.

"So, dinner?" He smiled again, taking her breath away.

"Um, sure," she stuttered.

"You're cute," he smirked making her heart do little flips.

Emerson appeared in the kitchen. "Mmmmm," she took in the smell of the pies.

"What do you think?" Neena asked nervously.

"These pies are amazing! Thank you so much! These will be perfect for my fundraiser." Emerson gave her a squeeze, her smile wide.

Neena suddenly felt shy.

"We're going to Maeve's for some chow. Do you want to come, Momma?" Gavin threw his arm around Emerson, dwarfing her as he did so. Neena hadn't realized how small she was until Gavin towered over her.

"No, you kids go. I have to get the house ready. Anna and Mona are coming for a visit and they're staying here for a few days."

"Anna is my sister," Gavin volunteered.

"You have a sister?" Neena was confused. She'd only ever known there to be the boys.

"Yes, we've kept it fairly quiet, but Sawyer had a daughter from a very brief relationship with Mona. It was years ago when we were broken up. Anna is a beautiful girl, and we want to keep her in our lives so they come and visit on occasion, and when we can, we go and visit them." Emerson explained.

"Oh... that's so nice!" Neena felt guilty for asking but was surprised that she hadn't heard about Gavin's sister before.

"Yes, it was a shock at first, but we've come to love her very much. Sawyer loved her and wanted to make sure she was taken care of, so we make sure she is. And we love on her every chance we get."

"We don't know how long she'll live," Gavin broke in, surprising Neena. "She has a lot of medical issues and ... honestly... everyone is surprised that she's made it this long. She's a bit older than Garrett and me, but she's strong. A lot stronger than anyone ever thought."

The pride in Gavin's voice was evident.

Neena smiled at the compassion in him, and she added that to his list of good qualities.

"Well, you kids should get to Maeve's. Tell her that I said, 'hello' and give her a hug for me." Emerson gave Neena a hug and then reached up to kiss Gavin on the cheek.

They waved their goodbyes and Neena followed Gavin outside where her beater car sat waiting.

"Do you want to ride with me?" Gavin offered pointing to his jeep.

"Sure." Neena imagined how the wind would make her hair fly around her head, making it even wilder than it already was.

As they rode to the Cathead, they chatted easily and Neena found herself more at ease when they reached the diner. As they settled into a booth, Neena could feel everyone's eyes on them.

She was afraid to look up.

She had underestimated what it would be like to walk into Maeve's with Gavin Grey, and she was terrified that if she looked up she would see the curious looks of the other diners boring into her.

"Are you okay?" Gavin whispered across the table.

"Yes." Her voice was barely audible as she buried her face in her hands.

"What's wrong?"

"I'm sitting at the Cathead with Gavin Grey. That's what is wrong." Neena could barely make out the words.

"Okay," Gavin chuckled, making Neena even more nervous. "But nobody cares."

"What? Of course they care. They're probably thinking, who's that girl with the crazy hair that he's sitting with?"

"I love your hair. It's beautiful." Neena could tell that Gavin was smirking again.

"Seriously, this is so embarrassing." Neena wanted to cry. She'd spent her entire life trying to hide from the sins of her mother, and a life without her. She could remember hearing the kids talk about her when she was in school, their whispers haunting her even years later.

Having dinner with Gavin Grey was just drawing unnecessary attention to herself.

Neena felt Gavin grab her hands and gently pull them away from her face.

"Look." He looked around the room at the other diners who were busy eating, drinking beer, and ignoring them completely. "Nobody is looking at us."

"God, I'm such a freak," Neena moaned.

"No, you're not. I get it. I've been dealing with this my entire life. This is what happens when the town is named after your family." Gavin laughed gently. "I know that it may be weird for you because of the whole 'Grey' thing, but my mom, grandma, brother and I are all pretty normal. You don't have to be freaked out by us. Momma has really taken to you and it's taken her years to be open to trusting other people, but she's so much happier now that she's done it. I guess... we just want to be your friend."

"But why? Why would you want to be *my* friend? I'm not anything special."

Gavin looked surprised, his eyes wide.

"Of course you are, Neena. Why would you think you aren't?"

"You don't even know me."

"Well... I'll tell you a secret. I had a crush on you in high school but you wouldn't even give me the time of day so I never tried to talk to you. I always thought you were ... incredible then." Gavin blushed.

Neena sat with her mouth open.

"I... I had no idea. I would've never talked to you in high school.

You were always surrounded by girls and friends and I was... not. I'm just ordinary, Gavin. I'm just a girl with a screwed up family life who is going to school and trying to make something of myself."

"That's why you need to be my friend, Neens." Gavin winked at her making her heart instantly flutter. "I'll help you see yourself for who you really are. That's what I do. I'm a carpenter. I look for and bring out the beauty in everything."

And just like that, Neena fell in love with Gavin Grey.

23

G ina

GINA WAITED FOR THEO TO GET HOME.

She needed him to take her to see Chloe.

Chloe had told her to stay home but Gina was anxious. The intense need to get to her dearest friend was like an unstoppable force she couldn't explain. Chloe had always been there for her, around every crazy turn, and she need to be there for her now.

Chloe had been there after Linc disappeared and they had grieved together, both hoping that he might return one day. She'd been there to support her during the days she didn't think she could make it through, when her parents had died and she had pretended not to care, and when she lost her first child in the womb, and for the birth of her other two.

She only remembered life without Chloe as dim and dark and couldn't imagine a world without her in it.

Gina had spent her entire life learning to control her emotions, but she wasn't sure she would be able to now. The mere thought of living without Chloe made Gina feel faint.

"Where are you, Theo?" Gina paced, pushing down the nausea that never seemed to subside. All she could think about was Chloe.

I need to get to Chloe.

The front door flew open and Gina ran to it, ready to race out of the door and jump in the car until she saw Theo's face.

"Oh God, Theo, is everything all right?"

His face was drawn, his handsome features tight.

His usually impeccable appearance was disheveled, and his face wore a sheen of sweat.

"Yes, I just... need to sit down for a minute. I'm sorry. We'll go in just a minute."

His breathing was abnormal as he struggled toward the couch.

"What happened? Do you need some water?"

Theo nodded.

Gina rushed to grab him a glass of water, her own concerns falling away for a brief moment.

"What... are you ... you're not hurt are you?" Gina handed him the glass of water and watched as he took it, his hands visibly shaking.

"I-I-I was rushing home because I wanted to get to you... and then... this huge truck came out of nowhere and nearly hit me head on. I swear that my life flashed before my eyes. I thought for sure I was dead." Theo's voice was low and monotone as though he was trying to believe the story as he told it.

"Oh God! But... you're okay?"

"Yes, I swerved just in time. If there had been a car in the other lane... I would be dead right now, Ginny. Gone! And then you and the kids... who would take care of you?"

Tears filled his eyes as he swiped at them impatiently. He had never cried in front of her before. He had never needed to, but it had been a difficult day, and the thought of leaving her forever had shaken him to the core.

She reached up tenderly and wiped his tears away. His vulnerability touched her heart in a way she had never imagined it would. He had never needed her before, but he did now.

She realized how strong he had always been for her without asking for anything in return and her heart softened.

Gina sat next to him and pulled him to her.

"Don't talk like that. It's okay. You're here now. You're safe, with me." She gently placed his head on her shoulder and held him as she stroked his thick dark hair.

He was her rock, the one who held it together, and as he leaned against her, absorbing her warmth and love, she suddenly felt like the strong one. They held each other for a long time, neither of them moving, afraid to break the spell.

As Theo's head rested on Gina's breast, his body tight against hers, he could feel the beginnings of a tiny baby bump and he prayed.

He wasn't even sure who he was praying to. He had never believed in a higher power, but he had watched his life flash in front him and realized he needed to be thankful to someone. He had been living life as a good father and husband, but there were days he didn't feel that was enough.

Like he was enough.

He realized as Gina held him in her arms that he was more than enough for her and his family. He was her world and she was his.

"Oh no! We should go." Theo startled. "You wanted to see Chloe."

Gina shushed him.

"She'll understand." Gina stood up and propped a pillow, settling him into the large soft couch. "You need to rest for a while, and then when you wake up, we can go."

Gina kissed him on the forehead, her lips soft and tender.

She sat next to him and stroked the side of his face as he closed his eyes, his other hand holding her free one. Her skin was warm, and as he breathed in her clean scent, his heart was full.

As his thoughts turned to Chloe, their friend, he understood Gina's sadness. His heart was breaking, too, at the thought of her illness and what would lie ahead.

He had been by his sweet mother's side while she fought for her life and it had been brutal. He had hidden his pain from Gina, who just had Lincoln at the time. His was a difficult birth and recovery, but she had refused a nanny, and he had made sure he shielded her from his suffering.

He realized now that he had hidden her from his entire heart as well, shielding him from his own fear and pain. Her presence was comforting as he closed his eyes and allowed himself to let his mind go just for a moment.

He had never been shaken up so badly, but he had also never been so close to death. As he dozed off, he felt her warm breath against his cheek.

"I'm here for you, Theo. I'll always take care of you just like you've done for me."

24

A bi

As they pulled down the long driveway, Abi admired the beautiful house that Chloe had been living in. She was ashamed that she had never been to visit since they had already been there a year.

Butterflies fluttered in her stomach as Dominic and Lexi talked non-stop.

"Whoa, this is a big house! Is Aunt Chloe rich, Mommy?" Dominic's deep blue eyes, so much like her own, widened, as they got closer to the house.

"Shhhh, Dom! That's not appropriate!"

"What's not appropriate?"

"Asking if someone is rich," Abi snapped impatiently, knowing her mom wouldn't like the question.

"Well, is she, Mommy?" Lexi's tiny voice yelled from the third row of seats.

"That's enough, Dominic and Lexi! Didn't you teach them any manners?" Anita glared at Abi.

Abi cowered in her seat as the large SUV came to a stop.

"Of course," she muttered under her breath.

"Grab the bags from the back kids! We're going to see Aunt Chloe," Anita barked.

Abi took a deep breath.

They carried grocery bags as they walked up to the house. Anita let herself in without knocking.

"We're here, Chloe," she called out to nobody.

The house was quiet.

"Go and find your sister," Anita pointed at Abi.

Abi walked through the quiet house. She wasn't surprised to find that it was immaculate. Chloe had always liked everything in order and the house reflected that.

Not one thing was out of place.

Abi shook her head imagining how horrified Chloe would've been walking into her apartment, where nothing matched and it always looked lived in.

"Chloe," she called out quietly.

"Abi?" Chloe's voice came from behind her, and Abi jumped.

She turned slowly, her heart in her throat.

"Chloe!" Abi cried out, grabbing her sister before she could stop herself. She squeezed her tight and held on.

"Oh!" Chloe paused for a moment before she hugged back. "I'm okay, Abs."

Abi began to cry, unable to stop herself, her emotions bubbling over.

"I'm sorry," Abi sobbed.

"I'm okay, Abs. Really, don't cry." Chloe stroked her sister's long thick hair.

Chloe was always jealous of how Abi didn't even realize how effortlessly beautiful she was, her long hair flowing down her back. Chloe had to work so hard to make sure she looked good while Abi did nothing. As she stroked her sister's hair, all of the resentment she had fell away and she found comfort that she was finally there.

"I-I-I'm a t-t-terrible sister. I'm so sorry." Abi tried to regain her composure. "God... I'm sorry."

"You make it impossible to be mad at you for completely ignoring me. You're such a brat." Chloe kissed the side of Abi's head as she held her tight.

"I'm home now. Apparently, for good, according to *your* mother." Abi grinned through her tears

"Yeah, well *your* mother is driving me crazy already." Chloe grinned back at their inside joke.

"Girls!" As though on cue, Anita yelled through the house for them.

Abi walked with Chloe to the kitchen.

"Aunt Chloe!" Dominic and Lexi cried out together, both running toward her and hugging her.

"Kids... stop! Aunt Chloe needs her space," Anita yelled sharply making the kids release her instantly.

"Sorry," Lexi looked like she was going to cry.

"You can hug me." Chloe grabbed both children and drew them toward her as Abi looked on gratefully.

"Humph," Anita uttered, disapproving.

"Relax, Mom," Chloe sighed.

Anita turned to put the groceries away, slamming cabinet doors as she did so.

"Where's Savi?" Abi asked, eager to see her niece.

"With her dad." There was a trace of sadness even though Chloe tried to sound casual.

"Are you hungry?" Anita interrupted.

"No, Brent is bringing me back some Won Ton Soup."

"You don't eat pork!" Anita looked alarmed.

"No, Mom. But I like the broth and I eat the dumpling without eating the pork."

"Oh—I didn't know that."

Chloe and Abi's eyes met as they smirked at one another. One of their favorite things to do as they had gotten older was to do things that would exasperate their mother.

Anita insisted on making a vegetable stir-fry as they waited for Savi and Brent to return. As she busied herself in the kitchen, Abi and

Chloe caught up as they sipped tea in the dining room where Anita couldn't butt in every two minutes.

"So, have you talked to that piece of shit ex of yours? Has he seen the kids?"

"No," Abi admitted.

"Don't be embarrassed, Abi. It's not your fault. Just like it's not my fault that Brent cheated on me. We just don't know how to pick'em."

Abi nodded.

"I just wish we would've talked when Todd was doing that to you. You shouldn't have gone through that alone," Chloe scolded her.

"And I should've been there for you when you found out about Brent."

"I haven't been a very a good sister," Chloe admitted. "I know you felt like I judged you."

"You did judge me," Abi blurted out without thinking.

Chloe's cheeks colored.

"You're right... I did. I thought you were too good for Todd. I never understood why you married someone like him."

"I felt the same about you and Brent," Abi spoke quickly, afraid she wouldn't get the words out before she lost her courage. "He's a slime ball. He actually asked to see my boobs once."

"What?" Chloe's mouth fell open.

"And before you ask, I didn't!"

"Oh God, I didn't think you would." Chloe's head was pounding.

"You and I have bad taste in men." Abi sipped her tea, wishing instead that it was a beer.

"I think we just... never thought we deserved much," Chloe said thoughtfully.

"No. I know I never did. Plus, I just wanted to get the hell out of here." Abi felt guilty that she hadn't thought about Chloe at all when she left. She'd never considered her sister at all.

"I don't blame you. I would've gone, too..."

"But you didn't want to leave in case Linc came back."

Chloe nodded, tears welling up in her eyes.

"You know, I thought I saw him once." Abi had never told Chloe, afraid to get her hopes up.

"You did?" Chloe's eyes were wide. "Why didn't you tell me?"

"I wasn't sure, and I didn't want to hurt you. I swore I saw him on Gina's wedding day, at the church. It was only for a split second, but I would've sworn at the time it was him."

"Oh my God, I thought I saw him, too."

"He was in a black suit," they said at the same time.

Chloe began to cry.

"Why would he show up and not say anything?" Chloe's tears spilled over before she could stop them.

"I don't know... I wish I could say something that made sense... but nothing makes sense."

"God, I just don't understand why he wouldn't talk to me. How could he be there and not say anything to me? To us?" Chloe fought to talk through her tears.

"I know. I'm sorry." Abi thought about how jealous she had been whenever Chloe had spent time with Linc. She had envied how they always seemed to be in sync, and when they looked at one another, it was as though nobody and nothing else existed.

Abi always wanted to have that for herself but never did.

"I wish Linc was here now. He would... make this better somehow. God..." Chloe sobbed, "I miss him. Even after all this time. You must think I'm a fool."

"No. No! I don't think that at all! I saw how in love you were. I... always wanted the same thing but..." Abi's voice trailed off.

"I'm so ... I spent so much time with him... I neglected you. I could've been a better sister to you growing up but...."

"No. Don't." Abi realized how much she wanted to help her sister. "I'm here... I know I haven't been, but I promise that I'll do the best I can to help make this better for you."

"I know you will, Sissy. Thank you."

Abi reached out and put her arms around her sister. They sat in silence, lost in their own thoughts.

All Chloe could think about was the handsome stranger she'd seen from far away in the black suit, and how somehow she had always known that it had been Lincoln.

25

SIX MONTHS LATER

C hloe

"I'M SORRY THAT I EVER LEFT YOU," LINC'S BREATH WAS WARM IN Chloe's ear.

"Mmmmm..." she murmured, inhaling his scent. There was nothing she loved more in the world than the way he smelled.

"Do you forgive me?"

"Yes." She did. She had waited for years, and when he finally returned, it was as though nothing had ever changed between them.

"I'll never leave you again. I promise."

Chloe's cheeks were wet with tears, the world suddenly spinning around her.

"Linc," she called out. "Linc!"

Her stomach heaved, nausea overtaking her as she stood up on wobbly legs and rushed to the bathroom just before the liquidy contents of her stomach emptied into the toilet bowl. She knelt over the cool porcelain no longer concerned with the germs as she rested her head on the seat, barely able to raise it.

"Chloe!" Abi's voice rang out in the quiet bedroom "Sissy."

Her voice got louder as she pushed open the door.

Chloe could feel her above her as she heard the water running and a cool towel being placed on her head.

"Dammit. You're sick again?" Abi's voice was agitated, though Chloe knew that it wasn't with her.

This was the second round of treatment, and while the doctor was hopeful, it was tearing her apart. The surgery to remove the tumor had been successful and the biopsy had come back malignant, but Chloe was determined to overcome it, as she was with everything.

Chloe nodded.

"Linc?"

"No, Sis, Linc isn't here. Remember, he's not anywhere." Abi put her shoulder under Chloe's armpit and raised her up easily, balancing her so that she could rinse her mouth out in the sink.

Chloe nodded again, averting her eyes from the mirror.

She couldn't look at herself. The haunted hollow eyes, her grey complexion, the bald head and bones sticking out where her flesh had once been. She hated the sight of herself.

"Can you eat something?" Abi walked slowly with her back to the bed.

Chloe shook her head.

"Linc."

"Another dream, Sis?"

Chloe nodded.

The dreams had been more frequent, and every time Chloe awoke to realize he wasn't there, her heart broke all over again.

"Savi wants to come in and read you a story. Is that okay?" Abi changed the subject. Lincoln hadn't been in their lives for such a long time, she wasn't even sure what she could say anymore. The worse Chloe got, the more she believed he was coming back, and Abi's heart could barely stand it.

Chloe nodded.

As Abi left the room, Chloe closed her eyes and talked to Lincoln as she often had over the years.

I know you're not really here and that you haven't been here for a very long time. But I need you now. If you can hear me at all, please know. I need you now.

Chloe knew that Abi thought she was losing it, but she was tired, and she didn't know how much longer she could hold on. The treatment was worse than the disease and she hated feeling sick all the time. With barely enough energy to stay awake, she couldn't even spend time with Savi without falling asleep, and she knew it broke her little girl's heart even though she was brave.

Every day, Savi came in and read to her until she fell asleep.

As the door to her bedroom opened slowly, Chloe could hear Savi breathing.

"Mommy," her voice was barely a whisper.

Chloe motioned for her to come closer. A tear squeezed out of the corner of her eye as she thought about the times she had been impatient with her.

"Your socks don't match, Savi. Are you blind?"

"You eat so slowly. You need to stop talking so much and eat faster. I'm not waiting all night for you to be finished."

"Please stop asking so many questions, Savi! You're making me tired."

Chloe would give anything to have those moments back.

Savi was a sweet girl, but as Chloe lie alone in her bed for weeks and months, she had come to realize that she had never appreciated her until now.

Chloe felt the weight of her tiny body climb on the bed and felt the brightness from the lamp as she clicked on the light.

"Are you okay, Mommy?" Savi's tiny voice was hopeful.

"Yes, sweetie. Mommy is okay. I'm just tired." She lifted her body and took a sip of the water that sat on her end table.

"Do you want me to read to you?" She showed Chloe the book she had brought with her.

"No, Sav. Just tell me what you've been up to if that's okay."

"Well, Auntie Abi made me and Dom and Lexi blueberry pancakes this morning. She said we had to be very quiet because you were sleeping and then Dom made noise, and Riley started barking, and Auntie got mad and put Dom in a time out."

Chloe smiled.

"Then, Nonny picked up Dom and Lexi to go to reading day at the library, but I didn't want to go because I hadn't see you yet and Nonny got mad but Auntie said I didn't have to go."

Abi is finally standing her ground. Chloe was impressed and surprised, even though she realized she shouldn't be. The past six months, Abi had been taking care of her more than Anita had, which Chloe was grateful for. Anita was efficient but Abi was kind.

She thought how much she had underestimated Abi all of their lives.

"That sounds like an interesting morning." Chloe struggled for the words.

"Yes. Then Auntie said I should read to you if you wanted me to because she said you are tired and will probably go back to sleep soon." Savi's big blue eyes were large as she peered into Chloe's face. "Are you tired, Mommy?"

"Yes, sweets. Mommy is tired, but I would love it if you would read to me now." Chloe put her arm around Savi, pulling her close.

Savi carefully opened her book, turning the pages with delicate hands.

Her face became very serious as she began to read, her voice mesmerizing as Chloe listened to the rhythm of Savi's voice. Chloe searched her memory to find one when she had ever read to Anita out loud but couldn't. The only memories she found were the ones where Abi had sat on her lap and read to her. Chloe had loved listening to Abi read the words so precise and perfectly, just as Savi was doing now.

"Do you like the story, Mommy?" Savi paused to look over at her.

"Yes, I do." Chloe smiled as she closed her eyes. "Thank you so much for reading it to me."

"You're welcome, Mommy."

Chloe thought how much Linc would've loved Savi. He had always talked about being a father.

"We'll have a beautiful kid, one day," he had said many times.

But Savi wasn't just anyone's kid. She was Chloe's. She didn't even consider that she was Brent's anymore since he couldn't bother to come around or help take care of her.

Chloe squeezed back a tear as she listened to Savi continue her story.

The same question had been haunting her for the past month.

Who would Savi be able to tell her stories to when Chloe was gone?

❦ 26 ❦

G ina

"GOD, YOU'RE SEXY." THEO WRAPPED HIS ARMS AROUND GINA AND placed his hands tenderly on her swollen belly.

"Oh, stop!" Gina swatted playfully at his hands.

At seven months pregnant, Gina was the most beautiful pregnant woman Theo could ever recall laying his eyes on. She glowed in her long black evening gown that accentuated her beautiful curves.

"I wish we didn't have to go to this charity dinner tonight, honey. You need to slow down."

"If I get any slower, I'll be dead, Theo. I already agreed to let you hire a housekeeper and a nanny. How much more do you want me to give up?" Gina kissed him on the cheek. It had taken her months to finally agree to have help in the house, and Theo was thrilled.

"You know what I mean. You have to make sure that our little munchkin in there is safe and sound, and so are you." Theo pulled her in close. "You know, you're still the most beautiful woman I've ever seen."

"You're too much!"

Theo loved that he could still make her blush.

Ever since their rough patch and Theo's near-death experience, they had been closer than ever.

Theo had persuaded her to see a therapist again to deal with her childhood and the disappearance of her brother. She had made him promise to accompany her when it became too difficult, not realizing that it would all be too hard to face.

They began to visit Dr. Libby regularly every week, always with a visit to the Cathead or Mizzen Mast after.

Theo joined her for every session because he knew that she would never allow herself to be happy and loved until she faced her demons, no matter how ugly they may be. Dr. Libby had been hesitant to allow him to sit in but when he saw how much Theo helped her, he allowed it.

The sessions were excruciating for both of them.

He had never understood how Gina had made it through her life without being haunted by what her parents had done to her until he realized how deeply she had buried it, in her art, in her physical activity, and ultimately in her quest to be perfect, refusing to let it define her.

He had developed a new level of respect for her as he listened to her recall how her mother had traded her innocence for drugs and her father had done nothing about it. It gave Theo rage he never knew existed within him, and it finally compelled him to seek therapy of his own so that he could cope with the mental images of young Gina being violated by men who were twice her age. If her parents weren't already dead, he knew without a shadow of a doubt that he would've found someone to kill them, if he hadn't done it with his own bare hands. The helplessness he felt as he learned more about Gina's suffering put him on the verge of despair.

Lincoln's disappearance still haunted him, but no matter how much money he invested, nobody could seem to find him. He was like a ghost, even though Theo knew in his gut that he had to be out there somewhere.

"Tell me about the night your brother disappeared." Dr. Libby had been working up to it even though Gina avoided talking about it every session.

Theo could feel Gina tense up. She knew it was coming. They had been circling around it for weeks, but she always stopped right before diving in. Dr. Libby knew that it was the main source of her pain.

"You'll have to face it. We're going to dig into this next week," he had warned, and he was true to his word.

"I... um... It was just an ordinary night." She locked eyes with Theo who put his hand out for her to hold.

"It was a normal night..." Gina cleared her throat. "Momma was high... Dad was off somewhere getting drunk. Linc had just gotten home from ... being with Chloe."

Gina's voice became thick as she sipped some water.

She cleared her throat.

"There was a knock on the door and Momma answered and let three men in. They were terrifying. One of the men... was familiar." Gina looked at Theo for reassurance and he knew instantly what she meant. It had been one of the men who had raped her, who her mother had traded her for so that she could have another supply of whatever her flavor of the week was. "At first I thought he was coming for me, but he wasn't."

Gina closed her eyes and tears began rolling down her cheeks.

"Momma called for Lincoln to come out. She handed him a duffel bag and then told the man he could take him. Lincoln fought..."

Theo could feel her squeezing his hand hard.

"Lincoln fought hard but then one of the men came over and grabbed me around the neck and put a gun to my head. 'I'll kill your little sister, but first I'll rape her right in front of you and then I'll kill her.' The man was serious, and we knew it. Momma stood there and didn't say anything. Then Lincoln stopped fighting and followed the man out the front door and I never saw him again. Momma told me that if I ever told anyone, Chloe, the police or even Daddy, that she would tell the man he could kill Lincoln. I believed her."

The air in the room was still.

"Jesus," Theo breathed.

"What happened after they left?" Dr. Libby's face was a blank slate.

"Nothing. Daddy came home a couple of days later and never even mentioned him. Chloe called the police and they came to the house, but they said he must've just run away and they didn't do anything about it." Gina spit out the words angrily.

"So, do you know where he went? Where they were taking him?" Dr. Libby asked gently.

"No. Momma and Daddy refused to talk about him, as though he never existed. When I finally got up the courage to ask a few weeks later where they had taken him, they got into a fight about it, and when they were done fighting, she turned on me. It was the worst beating I had ever gotten in my entire life, and after that ... I went to live with my aunt and uncle in Gilmore."

"Did you ever tell your aunt what happened?"

"She never asked." Gina buried her head in her hands and began to sob as the room remained quiet and they waited.

"I didn't know my aunt. Every time her husband looked at me... I felt violated, so I stayed away from him as much as I could. I ... didn't know that my momma's side of the family had a lot of money. She'd never talked about them our entire lives. A few days after I asked questions about Linc, their driver pulled up in front of our house and I got in the car and never saw my parents again. I didn't even get to say good-bye to Chloe..." Gina's voice trailed off.

"But you remained in touch with her?" Dr. Libby leaned in.

"Yes. I called her as soon as I could and we talked every day after. It was the only way either one of us survived Lincoln's disappearance, but I couldn't tell her what happened. I was too afraid that something would happen to her if anyone found out that she knew."

"I'm proud of you, Gina. This isn't easy." Dr. Libby smiled warmly at her. "We'll resume next week."

Gina nodded, her stomach in knots.

As they walked out of Dr. Libby's office, Theo's arm around Gina's waist, Gina was quiet.

"I'm proud of you, too, honey." Theo kissed her softly on the cheek but Gina pulled away.

"There's nothing to be proud of, Theo. I didn't tell either of you the worst of it ... what happened when I was at my aunt's house. I didn't tell you how I sold my soul to the devil."

"Gina, you were a kid. There's nothing you could've done ..."

Gina cut him off.

"You don't know me, Theo. I went from living with a crack whore mother and an alcoholic father to a mansion with the coldest people I've ever known. I went to a prestigious college and married a great guy... how do you think all of that happened? It happened because ... of what I did. I'm not a victim... I'm a fraud."

Theo stopped walking and turned Gina toward him, lifting her face toward his.

"Stop. You were a child! People should've protected you and taken care of you, but look at your life now. You have two beautiful children and one on the way and a husband who adores you. You have nothing to be ashamed of. You've done nothing wrong!"

Gina looked at him, a strange look in her beautiful green eyes that chilled him to the bone.

"You say these things don't bother you but you don't know everything. My sins will keep resurfacing over and over until one day, years from now, you'll look at me and you'll think differently. I promise you."

27

A^{bi}

Abi sat at the kitchen table and surveyed the mess.

The dishes in the sink were piled high; there was cereal from breakfast and milk on the counter, Lexi's crayons and coloring books were still where she had left them the night before even after being told repeatedly to put them away.

She didn't know how Chloe did all of this before she got sick, but she'd had a lot of help, Abi reminded herself. With the medical bills piling up, there was no nanny and no cleaning service.

There was just Abi.

Brent was barely in the picture any longer, popping in occasionally to take Savi to the zoo or the beach, playing the part of the hero dad. Abi would've thrown something at his head if it didn't lighten the load for at least a moment.

Overnight, Abi had become the single mother of three kids and caretaker to her ailing sister.

Anita had left most of it up to Abi, while she moaned on social media about her sick daughter and soaked up the sympathy and attention. Abi hated how believable she was and how people couldn't see behind Anita's ruse, but it had been that way their entire lives and she knew she shouldn't be surprised.

Or hurt.

Even though she always was.

Now it was just Chloe and Abi.

Abi marveled at how much Chloe had changed since her diagnosis. She had always held herself together so tightly, but Abi had observed a certain unraveling since she had become ill.

Abi was tired. She took a sip of her third cup of coffee and sighed. She needed to get out of the house. Chloe had mentioned Maeve's chicken noodle soup because she loved the broth, and Abi was craving a patty melt and some fresh cut fries from the Cathead.

"Chlo, I'm going to the Cathead now if that's okay?" Abi peeked her head into Chloe's room to check on her sister.

"That would be great, Abs." Chloe's voice was weak.

Abi placed the back of her hand on Chloe's forehead. No fever. She had been on high alert since the second treatment had landed Chloe in the hospital for a week, but she was tolerating this one better, even though she was sleeping a lot.

"Do you want anything else?" Abi kissed her softly on the top of her bald head.

"No, thank you," Chloe murmured.

Abi exited the room quietly and texted her dad to see if he would come over while she ran out. She'd had enough of her mom and appreciated that her father wouldn't ask a million questions or talk incessantly when he came over. Abi needed quiet and so did Chloe.

Forty-five minutes later, with her dad securely on Chloe-watch, she drove into town. She inhaled the salty air and for a brief moment felt the stress fall away.

As she parked and walked into the Cathead to order, she sat at the counter and grabbed a menu.

She wanted a patty melt but wondered if something else might catch her eye instead.

She looked over at a very tall man who sat a few seats over from her and admired his steaming chicken pot pie.

"Excuse me." She leaned over toward him. "Is that good?"

He looked startled that she was speaking to him.

"Um... yes. It's very good." He wiped the corner of his mouth with his napkin.

"I didn't know they had this here." Abi debated whether she wanted to order that or stick with her patty melt.

"It's the weekly special. I hate to admit it, but this is the second time I've gotten it this week." The man looked sheepish and Abi couldn't help but notice how handsome he was.

"It's only Tuesday," she laughed.

"That's why I was embarrassed to tell you," he smiled.

"I'm Abi." she stuck out her hand.

"I'm David. It's nice to meet you." He took her hand and shook it warmly.

"What's it going to be, kiddo?" Maeve Wynn's voice came across the counter.

"Hi, Maeve. I'm going to get a big bowl of chicken noodle soup and ... the chicken pot pie to go, please." Abi smiled, handing her the menu.

"Soup for Chloe, minus chicken?" Maeve asked, her blue eyes sympathetic.

"Yes, she loves your soup. It's the only thing she wants to eat these days."

Maeve nodded knowingly. She had her own share of suffering over the years and was sympathetic of others, too. Abi liked that about her.

"Is... something wrong with your sister?" David asked, hesitantly.

"S-s-she's got a brain tumor and we're going through her second course of treatment now." Abi said, putting her head in her hands. It never got any easier saying the words out loud.

David realized Maeve was watching him and tried to ignore it. She had been trying to set him up for years and he had always refused. He knew she'd be interested in his conversation with the young woman who had just happened to sit next to him and who was admittedly beautiful.

"You look like you need a break." David was unusually talkative, drawn to Abi for reasons he wasn't sure he understood. He had been alone for years, his relationship with Vanessa spanning nearly two decades of his life.

She had been his high school sweetheart and he had done every-thing he could to help her with her growing addiction. There were many times he was sure they had beat it, but she always went back.

She always left.

It wasn't until she left Jaden without explanation that he was finally able to be done with her.

He had kept his heart closed after that.

He had gotten to know Maeve from his many solo visits to the Cathead, and she had always been concerned for him. But he knew that even she would say that Abi was far too young for him.

Still he found himself attracted to her anyway.

"I could definitely use a break." She sighed. "But I'm not complaining because I love my sister."

"Of course you do," David smiled. "Just because you love her doesn't mean you can't use a break. Being a caregiver is exhausting both emotionally and physically."

Abi nodded. She was surprised at how comforting he was and how much she appreciated it.

"Are you from Grey's Harbor?"

"Yes, I grew up here but moved away for a while. I came back about six months ago because my life was falling apart and I needed some stability. I didn't want to face it then, but I needed to come back." Abi surprised herself with how comfortably she was talking with him. Something about the kindness in his eyes made her want to tell him things she hadn't told anyone else in a long time.

"Sometimes, there's no place like home." David thought about how he and Vanessa had always talked about leaving Grey's Harbor. Now he couldn't imagine raising Jaden anywhere but here.

They chatted until Maeve arrived with Abi's bag, and Abi was surprised at how disappointed she was that it was time to leave.

"Listen... if you ever want a break, my daughter is in the nursing program, and I'm sure she wouldn't mind coming over to sit with your sister. Maeve can vouch for us, she knows us pretty well." David had been searching for a reason to stay in touch with her and hoped desperately that Neena wouldn't mind him offering her services.

Abi looked surprised, but then her face fell.

"That's so nice of you to offer, but between my sister and I, we have three kids under the age of ten and that would be a lot to ask."

"She could bring my son, Jaden, who's also under the age of ten, and they could just have a little party. She's great with kids. I'm sure her boyfriend wouldn't mind tagging along either. He's a kid magnet." David thought about how Jaden had been immediately taken with Gavin, and he in turn with Jaden.

"Really? I mean... that would be ... great." Abi genuinely smiled for the first time since they'd met, and David marveled at how much it transformed her face making it even more beautiful.

He handed her his business card and wrote his cell phone number on the back.

"Seriously, just let me know. I'd just need a little notice because Neena is finishing school and doing her clinicals, but she's a great girl and would be happy to help."

Abi felt like a huge weight was being lifted off of her. The thought of just being able to go out to dinner, or get her hair cut made her feel giddy. Anita had offered, but there was always a price to pay, a reminder of how much she was doing for her, and Abi was too exhausted to feel indebted.

As David handed her his card, their fingers touched and Abi felt a spark of something she hadn't in a long time. Even though he was much older than any man she had ever dated, she felt drawn to him. He was classically handsome, though she was sure he had no idea, and a great listener.

She was sure he felt it, too, as he pulled his hand back a little too fast.

"I'll talk to you soon," she said, looking him directly in the eyes.

"That would be great." He flushed, uncertain when to break her gaze.

Abi walked out of the Cathead with her bag, unable to contain the smile on her face. It was the first time she'd remembered being happy in a long time.

Maeve watched her go with interest and smiled as she noticed the same look on David's face. It wouldn't be the first time a love connection was made at the Cathead, and God-willing, it wouldn't be the last.

❧ 28 ❧

Neena

NEENA HAD NEVER REMEMBERED BEING SO HAPPY.

She still had to pinch herself to believe she was dating Gavin Grey. He'd had the reputation of a ladies' man in high school, but he seemed content to be a one-woman man, and did everything he could to make her happy.

"I've never met anyone like you." Gavin surprised Neena with how much he liked her, and they had fallen hard for one another; their attraction mutual and strong.

The first time he kissed her, outside of the Cathead Diner for the entire world to see, she thought she was in a parallel universe. Nobody had ever even looked at her the way Gavin did, his hazel eyes intense as though they could see into her very soul.

"Gavin, everyone can see us," Neena had protested, his face inches from hers.

"I'm counting on it." With that he had covered her mouth with his, giving in to the weeks of waiting and wanting that had consumed them both. He had known the moment he laid eyes on her in the kitchen that he wanted to kiss her, years of longing realized.

Seeing her in his kitchen was like a dream come true.

Dating as a Grey was difficult at best. Garrett was finally dating a nice girl at college who didn't know who he was or what he was worth, but Gavin didn't have that luxury. He couldn't complain because he loved his life in the harbor, but he had been lonely, which is why he wouldn't move out of the Grey House. He knew that if he were alone too much, he would end up being too consumed with himself to allow happiness in.

His mom and grandmother had kept him grounded, and he loved being around them. He had nearly given up hope of meeting anyone he could love, until Neena.

"It's only been six months, Neens, but I... I want to know if you'd like to ... uh ... move in with me?" As they strolled down the beach hand in hand, Gavin finally found the courage to ask.

"You want me to move into the Grey house?" Neena's brown eyes were large as she looked into his.

"No, I was hoping you would want to move into our own place ... together. I love my mom, but I don't want to start a life with you while we live with her. I make enough money to have something of my own. I just never wanted to until now."

Neena's eyes lit up, but then her face fell instantly, her eyes welling up with tears. "I ... would love to ... but..."

"I already found the cutest little house. It's down the beach from Momma, but if you want us to look somewhere else..."

"That sounds wonderful, Gav. I love your Momma. But..."

"But..." Gavin lifted her chin toward him, grazing the scar that he loved to kiss.

"But I don't know that I can leave Daddy alone to raise Jaden. He needs me." Neena's voice trembled. She couldn't imagine leaving them to take care of themselves.

Gavin cleared his throat. "I... uh... talked to your daddy already and he is happy for us."

Neena looked at him in disbelief, sinking down onto the soft sand.

"You did? What did he say?"

"He said that he wants you to be happy and that it's time for you to live your own life. Now that you're almost done with school and you just have your clinicals... he wants you to focus on your life and your happiness. It's not as though we'd be moving away from Grey's Harbor. We'd be here, close."

Neena closed her eyes and took a deep breath.

"I can't believe he's okay with me moving out," she mused. She never considered leaving them before, but she was eager to start a new life with Gavin.

"Does that make you sad? If you're not ready..." Gavin stroked the side of her face.

"No!" Neena grabbed his hand and kissed his palm. "I never imagined that someone like you would ever love me. I just never considered that it could happen. I'm... happy."

"You deserve to be happy, we both do, and you are the person who makes me so happy. You are everything I'd ever hoped for and more, but if you want to think about it..."

"I don't need to think about it. I definitely want to move in with you. I want to be with you and have a life with you." Neena pulled him toward her and kissed him deeply. "I love you."

"I love you." Gavin kissed the tip of her nose.

Neena marveled at how he still made her heart flutter as she leaned against him, her head against his shoulder. She had never met anyone so perfect as Gavin Grey.

Her phone beeped and she ignored it, enjoying the moment.

They sat staring at the sunset, wrapped up in one another's love.

As they stood up to leave, Neena's phone beeped again.

She pulled her phone out of her purse. *Hello, doll.*

Neena's stomach dropped.

"What is it, Neens?" Gavin looked over her shoulder. "Doll? Who calls you that?"

"It's my mom." Neena hesitated. "Its like she can sense when I'm happy and then she swoops in to destroy it."

"Don't answer her then. Nothing and nobody can steal our happiness." Gavin's voice was protective.

"I know it's just..."

"You can't say 'no' to her, can you?"

Neena nodded. "I want to. She's done nothing but hurt me my entire life, but when she texts me its like *I'm* the addict. I don't want to answer but if I don't, I won't get it out of my head."

"Then answer her. Do it now and I'll help you."

Neena paused.

"No, I don't want to put you in the middle of all of this... mess."

"Neena, if we're going to do this then we're in it together. I'm here... for you."

Neena's phone beeped again with a series of question marks.

Neena hesitated then answered back. *Hi, Momma.*

She stared at the screen, waiting. *Hi, doll. When were you going to tell me the news?*

Neena's heart sank. *What news?*

She watched as the little dots floated on the screen.

The news that you're dating a rich boy. That you've managed to snag Gavin Grey.

❦ 29 ❦

G ina

AS THEY DROVE AWAY FROM THERAPY, GINA STARED OUT OF THE window silently.

"Are you okay, Ginny?" Theo tried putting his hand on hers but she pulled away.

"I didn't want to go to therapy but you made me. You said it would help but it's only making things worse. Now I have to face all of the things I've spent years trying to forget," Gina lashed out.

Theo was waiting for it.

She was often angry after a therapy session, and he let her vent until she had exhausted her frustration.

"It's good to get it out and deal with it. You're blaming yourself for things you shouldn't."

"How do you know I shouldn't? You weren't there! I know what I did, and now on top of everything else, I have to tell you what I did which is absolutely humiliating." Gina's face was red.

"I know what happened, Ginny. I know and I don't judge you for any of it. None of it was your fault."

"No? So, you don't blame me for letting my uncle have his way with me over and over so that he would pay for my college? He told me that it was the only way he was paying for any of it and he didn't give me a choice."

Theo froze.

He'd always suspected something terrible had happened but she had never told him. She had refused to invite him to the wedding, and when he died and left her a substantial amount of money, she didn't go to his funeral.

"Ginny, you were a kid who had just come from an awful situation and was thrust into another one. He was a grown man and took advantage of you!"

"How do you know? I knew better! I should've told someone! I should've..." Gina started to cry, quietly at first, but as her sobs grew louder Theo pulled the car over.

He pulled her into his arms and held her as her body shook and trembled.

"Shhhh." He whispered in her ear. "You were a child, Ginny. There is nothing you could've done. That man was a fucking bastard."

Theo could feel the rage welling up in him but he pushed it down and held Gina tight.

"God... how did you end up with me?" Gina sobbed.

"Ginny, I wouldn't want to be with anyone else."

"But my life... it's been awful and you're the one who has to deal with it. "

"I'm your husband and I want to be with you every step of the way. Look what you've done with your life, Ginny. You're beautiful, strong, compassionate, and you're an amazing wife and mother. You've overcome all of it, and you have a beautiful family and a husband who loves you. Ginny, others would've crumbled after a childhood like yours, but you've made a life for yourself." Theo stroked her back.

Gina clung to him, unable to imagine how he could possibly love her, yet somehow he did. He made her complete somehow.

Suddenly, she felt a sharp cramp in her stomach and she cringed.

"Are you okay?" Theo noticed the change in her expression immediately.

"I-I-I just felt a little twinge..." She rubbed her belly and held her breath for a moment waiting for it to pass.

When it finally did, she breathed a sigh of relief.

"It must've been the baby kicking," she smiled, wiping her eyes. She kissed Theo's cheek. "I'm sorry. This has been so difficult, and I know that I need to do this. I need to face my demons. Its good for all of us but... I'm terrified."

"What are you afraid of?" Theo pushed her hair behind her ear, his thumb lingering on her cheek.

"I'm afraid that you'll look at me differently and that it'll change your love for me when you know the truth" Gina admitted, her eyes avoiding his.

"Look at me." Theo lifted her chin until they were eye to eye. "Nothing could ever change my love for you. All of this has made me love you even more. Your strength and grace are unlike any I've ever seen. Don't ever worry about that, Ginny. I love you."

"I love you," Gina kissed his lips, his mouth warm and yielding against hers.

Another sharp pain radiated through her stomach and Gina groaned.

"What's wrong? Are you okay?" Theo's eyes darted to her stomach.

Gina tried to speak but the pain took her breath away.

"Gina..."

Theo grabbed his phone and called 911.

Gina tried to catch her breath but couldn't as the cramps intensified and shot white-hot pain through her entire mid-section. She could hear Theo's voice talking frantically to the 911 operator but couldn't concentrate on his words.

The agony was too great, and she felt like her head was disconnected from her body. She started to sweat, and as hard as she tried to make her mouth move to form words, she couldn't.

"Gina." Theo repeated her name, willing her to talk.

Theo watched in horror as her pants began to turn crimson. As the sirens drew closer, Gina's face began to turn white.

"What are you feeling?" Theo tried to hold her hand as she writhed in pain.

"Stomach... ripping..."

"Oh God... I'm right here, Ginny, I won't leave you. I'm right here."

Gina nodded, her eyes closed as she tried to catch her breath.

"The—" she tried to speak.

Theo leaned in so that her lips were pressed against his ear.

"I love you," she whispered.

The bright flashing lights of the ambulance appeared in the rearview mirror distracting him for a moment. When he looked over at Gina he was horrified to see that she was unconscious, her mouth open and her face slack.

"Ginny, wake up! Wake up!" Theo cried out.

There was a knock on his door, and he turned to see the paramedic peering in. As he opened the door his words came out in a rush.

"Please, help my wife. I don't know if she's breathing. She's pregnant!"

The next few moments were a blur of movement and activity as they asked Theo questions, often needing to repeat them. He refused to take his eyes of Gina as they checked her vitals, fitted her with oxygen, and hoisted her onto the stretcher and into the ambulance.

As he jumped into the back of the ambulance, he watched the paramedics work on Gina. Their efficiency and concern calmed him, but as the urgency in their voices grew, he knew that his wife and baby were in grave danger.

Lincoln and Leo!

Theo quickly texted Abi and asked if she could get the boys from school without telling her the reason. He knew that she had enough on her mind with Chloe and had no idea what he should tell her. The boys were always up for a play date with Savi, Dom, and Lexi. He felt bad asking but she was the only one he could trust in case something was to happen. His stomach flipped at the thought of giving Linc and Leo bad news about their mom as he quickly pushed the thought from his mind.

He couldn't allow himself to think about the boys losing Gina now.

As the sound of the sirens wailed, all Theo could do was pray.

Life without his Ginny wasn't an option. They were closer than ever, and he finally felt as though she was able to find peace in her life. The only thing she was missing in her life was her brother, but Theo didn't know if he was even alive any longer.

He held her limp hand in his as he bowed his head.

The paramedics had finally stabilized Gina and observed her carefully, but her vitals were weak. They wanted to give Theo more hope than he already had but they couldn't. They had seen this situation many times before and the outcome wasn't often favorable.

As they pulled up to the hospital, the doors flew open and Theo was surprised to see a team of white coats waiting for them. They rushed Gina out of the ambulance so fast; Theo didn't have time to think.

Someone in scrubs ushered him into an empty waiting room.

"We'll come and get you as soon as we know what's happening."

Theo stood in the middle of the room, tears streaming down his face. He wiped his eyes and took a deep breath.

He was always the optimistic one and he needed to hold himself together. He had to, for himself, for Gina, and for the kids. If he didn't, nobody else would.

"I love you," he whispered, willing her to hear him.

Everything is going to be okay. I promise. It's going to be okay.

𖧷 30 𖧷

C hloe

Chloe awoke, startled from the noise on the first floor.

Usually Abi made sure the kids were quiet and occupied, and they were unusually loud.

She sat on the edge of the bed and assessed herself. Aside from being tired, she felt good. Better than she had for her past treatments. She hoped that it meant it was working this time.

She took a deep breath and stood up, happy to note that her legs felt fairly strong underneath her. As she made the journey downstairs she cursed Brent for choosing such a big house. He was still paying the mortgage which was the least he could do since he'd apparently moved in with his new girlfriend and completey abandoned her and Savi.

As she neared the first floor the sound of children screaming and laughing grew louder.

Chloe could hear Abi hissing in a loud whisper "Be quiet!".

Her eyes widened as she saw Chloe come around the corner.

"Oh, Chlo! I'm so sorry. Did we wake you?"

Chloe counted heads and realized there were two more than usual.

"Why are Linc and Leo here?" Chloe ignored Abi's question.

"Um..." Abi pointed to the living room and motioned for Chloe to follow her.

"What's going on, Abs?" Chloe knew in her bones that something was wrong.

"Okay, please sit down."

"No! I'm not sitting down. What's going on?" Chloe's heart was beating hard in her chest.

"S-s-something happened with Gina. I don't know exactly what, but Theo asked me to get the boys and all I know is that she's at the hospital."

"How long ago was this? Why didn't you wake me?" Chloe snapped, going into panic-mode.

"Theo made me promise not to. He said that he wasn't sure what was happening and that he would let me know as soon as he knew more. He called when I was picking food up for us and I went straight from the Cathead and picked all of the kids up. Dad is still downstairs."

"Oh God, the baby..." Chloe's hand flew to her mouth." Is the baby all right?"

"I don't know, Chlo."

"I need to go and see her, right now!"

"I knew you would say that. Mom is on the way to help Dad watch the kids and I ordered pizzas for dinner. She should be here any moment."

As though on cue, Anita's voice rang through the house.

"Girls! I'm here! Where are you?"

Abi held her breath, waiting for the inevitable criticism that always came when her mom entered a room.

"There you are! These children are so loud. Abi, why are you allowing them to make so much noise? As a mother you would think you'd have more control. Goodness!" Anita's scowl was familiar. Abi tried to pretend that it didn't annoy her and she helped Chloe off the couch.

"Thanks for coming, Mom."

"I don't think it's a good idea for you to take Chloe to the hospital. You don't even know what's happening."

Abi rolled her eyes at Chloe, knowing Chloe would never agree to stay home.

"Mom, I'm going!" Chloe's tone gave no room for argument.

"Fine. What do I know? I'm just the mother." Anita gave Abi a dirty look and turned on her heel.

"Well, now that we've settled that." Abi smiled at Chloe.

"I just need to change and wash my face and I'll be ready." Chloe started up the stairs. "I don't need help."

Abi nodded. She hesitated as she made her way toward the kitchen to let her mother know she had already ordered pizza.

"Sissy, how long will we have Linc and Leo?" Anita asked.

"I don't know, Mom. It just depends on how Gina is doing. They don't have any other family, so we're it."

"You would think with the money they have that the nanny could..."

Abi cut her off, whispering under her breath. "They need to be with family right now."

Anita's eyes grew wide. She wasn't used to Abi speaking up and she closed her mouth, drawing it into a straight line and saying nothing else.

Abi checked in on the kids and kissed Dom and Lexi on the head.

"I'm ready," Chloe appeared, dressed casually in a long sweater and jeans.

Abi was impressed that even during chemo her sister could manage to look put together.

"Are you going to see our Mommy and Daddy?" Linc asked Abi.

"Yes," Abi knelt down so that she and Linc were eye level. She marveled at the depth of his dark eyes, just like Theo's.

"Give Mommy a hug and tell her that I love her, and Daddy too."

"Yeah, me, too," Leo echoed.

"I will. I promise." Abi gave both boys a smile. Even though she hadn't spent much time with them over the years, she remembered when they were born. They were the first babies she'd ever held, and she'd always had a soft spot in her heart for them.

As they left, Anita gave both girls a quick hug.

"Don't be long," she warned.

The sisters ignored her comment as they walked out of the house. The drive to the hospital was silent, each wrapped in their individual thoughts.

Chloe's heart raced, as they got closer.

"Are you okay?" Abi placed her hand on Chloe's as they pulled into a parking spot outside of the emergency room.

"I just need to see her." Chloe's voice was desperate.

"You will," Abi promised.

The attendant at the desk barely looked up as Abi asked where they could find Gina.

"Room twenty-two."

She buzzed them back and as they searched for room twenty-two they heard the rich timbre of Theo's voice. They walked into the room and Chloe's eyes immediately filled with tears at the sight of Gina's motionless body, her face pale.

"I don't understand," Theo said to a fresh-faced doctor who barely looked older than Abi, her long red hair pulled into a long braid revealing a pale, pretty freckled face.

"The ultrasound shows that the placenta has separated from the uterus. The good news is that the bleeding has finally stopped, but baby and mom's vitals are concerning. We're waiting for a couple of test results to come back but we may have to do a Caesarean section within the hour."

Chloe gasped, her hand flying to her mouth. Abi put her arm around her sister's waist to steady her.

"What does that mean? The baby is only seven months... is that old enough? Is Gina going to be okay?"

"The baby will need to go the NICU and we'll do all we can to make sure that all goes well. We're going to make every effort to make sure they both come out of this healthy and strong. I promise you that."

Theo turned to the sisters, his eyes filled with tears.

Chloe looked at her friend, a thick knot in her stomach.

"I'm sorry I don't have better news. We're monitoring them both closely and will let you know as soon as we know what we're doing. I'll be back to have you sign consent forms." The doctor nodded at the sisters and left the room.

Chloe knew that if Abi wasn't holding her that her legs would give out.

She looked down at Gina and allowed the tears to flow down her cheeks. "I'm here, Gina... I'm here. I love you. Everything is going to be okay!"

Abi pulled Theo toward them and they huddled together, staring at Gina in disbelief.

As the tubes snaked in and out of her body, cords hooked up to monitors that flashed and beeped, Gina's chest rose and fell peacefully, her eyes closed.

Theo placed his hand on Gina's swollen belly and held back a sob.

"It's going to be okay, Theo. We have to believe that everything is going to be okay." Abi tried not to allow her voice to betray the fear she felt deep in her heart.

Chloe nodded.

"Theo, lets get some coffee really quick. I saw some in the hall." Abi lightly touched his arm.

Theo looked at her dazed.

He nodded, allowing Abi to guide him out of the room.

Chloe sat down next to the bed and held Gina's hand in hers.

"Gina... it's Chlo. I'm here for you. You may have this baby today and that's okay. If he or she needs to be born now, then it'll be fine. Don't worry. Abs, Theo and I are all here. For you." Chloe's voice trembled.

Gina lay motionless, the machines beeping around her, the rise and fall of her chest the only response.

"You need to stay strong. You have babies who need you." Chloe tried to make her voice strong but faltered.

As Theo and Abi pushed back the curtain, the machines began to beep faster.

Two nurses flew into the room and began checking the monitors fervently.

"You have to leave the room right now! Please go to the waiting room!" the older nurse with an unpleasant expression barked at them.

"What's happening?" Theo's voice was edged with panic.

"Please. Leave!" the older nurse repeated.

As the red-haired doctor pushed into the room, another nurse entered and ushered them out, walking them into a private room off of the main waiting room.

"What's going on?" Chloe cried angrily.

"I'm sorry but it looks like their heart rates were dropping. We need to give the team time to take care of them." The nurse's kindness caught Chloe off guard.

"What does that mean?" Theo asked, his heart sinking.

"I don't know yet," the nurse smiled sympathetically. "I wish I could tell you more but I can't. I don't want to give you bad information. I'll come back as soon as I know more."

"Are they going to die?" Chloe asked the question they were all thinking.

"We're going to do the very best we can to make sure that mom and baby are healthy. I'll be back as soon as I know more." The nurse closed the door gently behind her.

Theo let out a deep breath that also sounded like a low cry.

Chloe buried her head in her hands, her body shaking in silent sobs as Abi wrapped her arms around her.

"It's going to be all right," Abi whispered as she held Chloe tight. "It has to be."

❧ 31 ❧

G ina

GINA'S EYELIDS FELT AS THOUGH THEY WERE CEMENTED SHUT.

As desperately as she wanted to open them, despite every effort, she could not.

There always seemed to be a flurry of activity around her, and try as she might, she couldn't move her body in any way, not even a finger. She could feel herself being poked and prodded, her eyelids being lifted, her pulse being taken, but she was unable to let them know that she was in there.

Fear gripped her tight and all she could think about was her baby, the helplessness welling within her.

She had been working so hard to get to a place where life finally made sense. She had been going to therapy to face her demons head on. Dr. Libby had made her confront every ounce of her pain. The first time Momma had sold her for drugs ... the fear ... the horror ... the shame.

She had never imagined that her first time would be that way. She never knew any other way. She had never known a man who didn't just want to use her, like the men her Momma made her be nice to, or even her uncle ... until Theo.

Theo, who had loved her even though it had taken her months to let him touch her, a year to have sex with her. He had seen that she was broken and imperfect but he had taken his time, promising to love her no matter what, and he did.

She had been the one to put impossible expectations on herself to be perfect.

Theo had loved her in spite of herself, and more.

She wanted to tell him that she understood now. It had taken years, and a lot of therapy, and the consistency of his love, but she saw it now. She saw him so clearly.

Theo.

He and Chloe had saved her. When Lincoln left, she was alone, and even though it wasn't his choice, she was angry with him. Why didn't he fight? Why didn't he refuse? She knew that the man had a gun to her head but didn't he know how much she needed him?

Didn't he understand? And why didn't he come back? Surely, he was a man who could make his decisions by now and could've come back for her and Chloe. Chloe never loved Brent, at least not the way she loved Linc. There was only one explanation for why he didn't return, and Gina couldn't accept that.

Her Lincoln couldn't be gone forever.

Chloe!

Gina could hear Chloe's voice through the fog. She would've recognized that voice anywhere. Husky and always in control. It was as though she had been born dignified. Even when they were teenagers and her parents smacked her around for no reason, she remained restrained. Abi fought back, but Chloe was a different story. Chloe just took it and moved on.

That's what Chloe always did. She took the shit life handed her, even her cheating husband and awful fucking tumor, and moved on. It had always served her well.

"It's going to be okay. I'm here and I love you." Chloe's voice floated through her ears, like music.

They had been there for each other when their children were born, and when they fought with their husbands. When one of them was sad, or tired, or angry, or confused, the other either listened or answered back for the things they couldn't do for themselves.

When Chloe was at her lowest, kicking herself for not being perfect, Gina reminded her time and again that she was enough.

"Don't listen to anything your asshole parents say. You're perfect, Chlo! Don't ever forget it," Gina would say.

What would Chloe do if she were no longer there? Who would remind her best friend that she was perfect when she needed to hear it the most?

She hated that Theo had been crying. She could hear him, but she couldn't console him. He was so sad, but she wasn't in pain. She would tell him when she woke up.

If...

She knew she shouldn't think about *if* but the doctors and the nurses seemed frantic. She knew she couldn't give up now. She had her baby to think about even though she wasn't sure if her baby was there anymore.

Everything felt different now and she was beginning to feel very tired, her body heavier than ever.

She just wanted to let go of her mind and body and go to sleep and stay asleep for a long time, until she was caught up. She just wanted to go, although she wasn't sure where she was going. She just didn't know if she could fight any more.

She was beyond exhausted.

She felt her body being lifted and set down on a hard table, even more activity surrounding her than ever before.

More voices surrounded her asking for instruments and vitals, and statuses that didn't make sense. Her body felt cold.

Very cold.

She could hear beeping, and pulling, and it felt as though her stomach was being tugged and pulled even though there was no pain. She heard a voice say, "She's not breathing" and she wondered who wasn't breathing. Gina was sure that she was still breathing even though she began to feel as though she was floating away.

Crying!

She could hear the sound of a baby wailing in the distance and a voice full of relief," She's breathing! Thank God. Take her to the NICU, now!"

The baby crying sounded like when Lincoln and Leo were born. The short, staccato, surprised cries of new life that sounded like betrayal, once they realized they were no longer in the nice warm womb. Every time Gina heard that sound, even years after the boys were born, it made her yearn for those first few weeks of their lives.

She knew that meant her daughter was finally safe in the world.

"We're losing her," another voice said even further away. "Keep working! Gina, hang in there."

But Gina was tired. More tired than she had ever been.

"Come on, Gina. Your daughter was just born. Don't you want to meet her?"

Gina did, but she knew she was in good hands. Theo would take excellent care of her and Chloe would help.

"Gina, dammit! Come on, let's find a pulse. Why is there so much goddamn blood?"

Gina knew they were doing their best, but she was ready to go.

Maybe she would see Lincoln.

Maybe he was waiting for her.

"Gina! I know you're in there. Your family needs you."

Gina felt herself fading even further, beautiful silence filling her head and ears.

She knew she should fight but there was nothing left in her any longer as she floated toward the white emptiness that called out to her. Everything was going to be as it should, and as she disappeared, all of the years of pain and struggle began to as well.

In that last moment, Gina was filled with a sense of calmness and peace she had always searched for but had never known, and for the first time ever, she found peace.

32

N eena

NEENA HAD NEVER EXPERIENCED LOSING A PATIENT.

It was only her first week on the maternity unit and this case was especially difficult. A young mother with a placental abruption, only twenty-eight weeks into her pregnancy.

Neena felt helpless but followed the instructions given to her, and when the baby was born successfully, she and her nursing instructor were part of the team that rushed the baby to the NICU.

As they left the room, she could hear the surgeon urging the young mother to hold on. Neena said a quick prayer, hoping that she would hear good news when she asked about her, later.

She had always had a specific fondness for babies and decided early on that she wanted to be a neonatal nurse but wasn't prepared for how it would feel to watch a young mother fight for her life.

She'd already spent many hours working between the maternity ward and the NICU and loved both. It was hard work, but she knew that she was meant to do it.

She had immediately fallen in love with the Davidson baby. She was beautiful with her dark hair and eyes, and even though she was early, she was strong, her vitals steady.

Several hours later, when a handsome man in his thirties entered the NICU, Neena knew immediately that this was the baby's father. His red-rimmed eyes and tear stained face gave away his grief, and she hoped with everything inside of her that his expression didn't mean what she thought it did. She fought down the lump in her throat.

"I'm Theodore Davidson." His voice was barely audible.

"Mr. Davidson. I'm Neena." She smiled, hoping it might give him some comfort.

"Is this... her?" he asked, peering through the incubator. His eyes were glazed over and Neena wondered if he was really able to see her through his pain.

"Yes," Neena gave him a smile. "She's beautiful, isn't she?"

The man nodded, unable to speak.

"Do you... do you have a name for her?" Neena was afraid to ask.

The man nodded.

He looked like he might faint as Neena moved a chair close to the incubator and gestured for him to sit.

"Is there something I can help you with?" Neena asked, looking around for help in case she needed it.

The man shook his head as he buried his face in his hands.

"She's gone," he cried, his voice hoarse. "My wife is gone."

"I'm so sorry." Neena could barely get the words out as he confirmed what she'd already suspected.

"I'm so sorry," she repeated unable to think of anything else to say.

"Is... she... the baby... is ..."

"She's doing well. She's strong. So far, there are no obvious complications other than her lungs need time to develop." Neena felt a strange pride in telling him that.

He nodded as he wiped his face. "Her mother... would be so happy."

Neena nodded.

He squinted his eyes and peered in at the tiny face.

He teared up as he stared at the tubes that weaved in and out of her nose. Neena watched as he searched her face and she wondered what he was looking for.

Suddenly, his eyes grew bright and a smile crossed his face for the first time since he'd entered the room.

"Ah, there it is," he whispered to nobody in particular.

"I'm sorry?" Neena moved in closer trying to see what he did.

He pointed to her face.

"Do you see the tiny mole on her cheek? My wife has... had... the same mole in the exact same place." He marveled at the similarity.

"That's wonderful," Neena said, fighting tears.

Theo had just kissed that mole for the last time as he said goodbye to her.

He thought about the last few hours of his life and wished he was just in a horrible dream. He hadn't been prepared for Gina to leave him. Even if she had lived until ninety he wouldn't have been ready. When the red-haired doctor came out and gave them the grim news, he and Chloe had clung to one other in disbelief.

The baby had made it but Gina hadn't.

The doctor was sincerely saddened, which gave Theo comfort. She seemed just as devastated when she explained how the shock had been too much on Gina's body and that they had done everything they could, but it was too much.

Theo stared at the doctor and wondered if he was caught in a bad dream and desperately wished he could wake up. How could his vibrant, beautiful, kind-hearted wife truly to be gone?

He wasn't ready to say goodbye to her yet. How could he be?

He wanted to feel something for the baby as he stared at her, but his heart was a tangle of pain and anger. As much as he wanted to feel love, it remained out of reach.

As Neena watched him, she felt her heart breaking and wondered if she could do this time and again. How could she watch such suffering and pain? She wondered if she was strong enough and if it was worth it, if she was worthy of being there for her patients' most private and intimate moments. She wasn't sure.

"Were you there?" Theo's question surprised her.

"I'm sorry. I'm not sure what you mean." Neena asked, her heart sinking.

"Were you there when the baby was born?"

"Yes, I was. I've been with her from the beginning. She's a fighter."

"Oh, good." Theo seemed relieved.

He turned his attention back to the baby. She had fallen asleep and Theo watched the rise and fall of her tiny chest, slowly mesmerized. He remembered watching Lincoln sleep for hours at a time, completely in awe that he had helped create such a perfect little person.

How will I do this without Gina? How will I tell Lincoln and Leo that their mother has died?

The questions came fast and furious, with no answers. Gina would know how to handle this. She had been working through hard things her entire life, but Theo had no experience with any of it. How was he going to make it through without her strength?

"How long will the baby be in here?" The question suddenly came to him.

"It will depend on how she does. I can't give you a definite answer yet." Neena had given the answer she knew her instructor would want her to give.

"Oh... of course."

"Is there someone I can call for you? Is there someone else who you want to be here?" Neena was concerned for him.

He thought about Chloe and how pale and devastated she was after the news. He knew that Abi needed to take her home.

"No, thank you." He shook his head. He wanted his mom more than anyone, but she was no longer there. His father had remarried only four months after she died and he barely spoke to him any more. He was unable to get it out of his head that he must've been sleeping with his receptionist before his mom passed to have married her so quickly.

He stared at the baby. With Lincoln and Leo, they knew the baby's gender before they were born. Gina had insisted knowing, but with their third, they decided to wait until she was born.

"There are few surprises left in the world. Let's just wait and see." Gina had uncharacteristically suggested, and Theo had agreed.

They had talked endlessly about names but had never agreed on one. Gina wanted to wait until they met the baby before they named it.

He wanted the baby to have a name that Gina would have loved.

"Francis Gina Davidson. That's the baby's name," Theo said to Neena, unsure if she had ever asked.

"That's a beautiful name." Neena smiled.

"We'll call her Frannie for short. Francis is her best friend's middle name, and Gina was... my wife." Theo explained.

Neena wrote it on the baby's chart.

"Frannie it is then."

"Hi, baby Frannie," Theo whispered, warmth spreading through his chest.

There it was, the love he had been hoping would find him. As he thought about Gina, he knew that she would be proud of him for allowing it in so quickly.

"It's what I love about you the most," she had said to him once.

"What is it?"

"Your giant heart and its capacity for tremendous love." She had kissed him as he basked in the compliment.

He thought about her as he stared at the tiny puckered fingers and soft sweet cheeks of his newborn daughter.

Gina, I won't let you, Frannie, or the boys down ever. I'll love and care for them just like you would've. I promise.

33

C hloe

Chloe despised wearing all black.

She stared at herself in the mirror and hated how washed out and sallow she looked. The dark circles under her eyes were unmistakable. There wasn't enough makeup in the world that would cover them.

She couldn't believe she was going to Gina's funeral.

Her Gina.

The only person in the entire world who understood her. She never had to pretend with Gina because Gina never judged her. Even when she was too hard on Savi, or too focused on her career, or married the wrong man.

Even when she didn't like herself, Gina was always in her corner.

Life without Gina was unimaginable.

"Are you almost ready, Chlo?" Abi stood in the doorway of her bedroom, hesitant.

"Yes." Chloe's voice was hoarse from crying. The last few days had been a blur and Abi knew better than to ask Chloe if she was all right.

She already knew the answer.

Surprisingly, their parents had volunteered to watch Abi's children without being asked. They had agreed they were too young to attend a funeral, even though Savi insisted on going to say goodbye to Aunt Ginny.

Chloe reluctantly agreed.

The drive to the funeral home was somber and even Savi was unusually quiet. She seemed to understand the gravity of their loss. Aunt Ginny was one of her favorite people and she understood she would never ever get to see her again. She was beginning to understand loss since she barely got to see her Daddy, either.

Nonny told her that people die all the time and that she needed to get used to it so Savi decided she would be a big girl. She could tell her momma needed her and she wasn't a baby anymore.

Bill and Fiona Henderson, fourth generation Grey's Harbor, owned the Henderson's Funeral Home. They were a kindly couple in their seventies who handled the arrangements for Gina's funeral with a combination of grace and compassion.

As Chloe and Abi stepped into the parlor with Savi right behind them, Chloe felt as though she might faint.

"Can I get you a glass of water, dear?" Fiona Henderson stepped out of the office and immediately came to Chloe's side.

"Yes, please." Chloe's throat was dry.

Fiona hurried off as Abi grabbed Chloe's arm. "Are you going to be okay?"

"No, Abs. I don't think that I'll be okay ever again." Chloe's voice was flat. Savi reached up shyly and grabbed her hand.

Chloe looked down at her beautiful daughter and attempted a smile.

"I love you, Savi. Momma is going to be fine." She knew that she didn't sound convincing, but she thought she should say something.

Fiona appeared with a bottle of cold water and opened it, handing it to Chloe. "Mr. Davidson is already here with his boys. Do you want me to show you the way?"

Chloe nodded.

She wasn't sure if she could do it as she concentrated on putting one foot in front of the other.

They walked down the short hallway to the room where the service was going to be. The large sleek casket sat in the front of the room, and Chloe felt the bile coming up in the back of her throat.

The smell of flowers was overwhelming. It looked as though every residence in Grey's Harbor had sent an arrangement.

Chloe was glad everything would be over after today. She knew that Gina would never want a large church service or multiple visitations. She would want things to be simple and that's what Theo had done. One service, no visiting hours, and family only at the cemetery. Theo and Chloe knew that Gina would be satisfied.

No fuss.

But Chloe also knew that Gina wouldn't want to be dead! Chloe forced herself to breathe.

"Chlo!" Theo looked relieved to see them as they entered the room.

The casket was still open, temporarily. He had requested that it be closed for the service, which he knew Gina would want. She would never want people to see her that way.

"Theo," Chloe walked into his embrace and they held each other tight. "How are you holding up? How are the boys?"

Both boys stood close by in dark suits with their hair perfectly combed. They both wore sneakers, which made Chloe smile. Gina would've wanted them to be comfortable and sneakers were the ultimate form of comfort. She looked at them, as they bravely stood by, straight as soldiers, seemingly afraid to move.

Savi joined them and Chloe stifled a sob.

If this round of treatment didn't work, Savi would be standing next to her casket within the year. Chloe had tried not to think about it but she knew it was true. It was supposed to be her in the casket and not Gina.

"Don't..." Theo looked at her as though he knew what she was thinking.

"They can't all be without their mother's, can they?" Chloe searched his eyes for an answer.

"You're going to be okay. Savi needs you and now the boys will, too. Who is going to tell them stories about her and their Uncle Lincoln? They need you." Theo put his hand on her arm. "You're not going anywhere."

Chloe hoped it was true as she stared at Gina in the casket.

Theo had picked out her favorite dress. The beautiful pink one she had loved so much. When she was alive, it had looked perfect on her but now it looked as though it was on someone else. While they had done their best with her make up and hair, Chloe knew it wasn't her. It couldn't be her. She was no longer in that shell of a body, unable to sustain it any longer.

She was glad it was going to be a closed casket.

She stared at the large picture of her next to the casket. It was the one taken on her last birthday, when Theo had surprised her. The look of joy and laughter on her face made her glow. A thoughtful partygoer had snapped the moment on their phone and sent it to Theo soon after. It became one of his favorite photos of her.

They stood in front of the casket in silence.

Chloe began to cry, her chest heaving. Abi held her tight, tears running down her cheeks.

The door to the room opened behind them, but they barely noticed as a tall man in a dark suit entered the room, each lost in their own grief.

Theo moved silently in front of the casket and stared at Gina's face. The moments of finality were creeping upon him and he knew that it wouldn't be long until the Henderson's would come in and close the casket. He knew that Gina wouldn't want everyone to see her this way, but he couldn't bear the thought of never seeing his wife's beautiful face again. He tried to tell himself that she was just sleeping, but when the permanence of his loss was looming ahead as he felt his throat constrict.

"Would it be okay if I said good-bye?"

Chloe froze.

She hadn't heard that voice in many years but she would've known it anywhere.

Theo turned around, angry with the intruder who was trying to steal their valuable time with Gina before everyone else arrived. "Who are you? Why are you here? The funeral isn't for another hour."

"I'm sorry. I'm ..."

"Lincoln," Chloe finished for him.

When she last saw him, he was a boy, but he had grown into a man, and he took her breath away. She would've never believed it if he wasn't standing six feet in front of her, his gorgeous eyes with their long lashes, staring at her, unwavering. He filled out his black suit in a way she had never imagined he could, his thick blond hair unruly but perfect, just as she remembered. He had a new scar just below his right eye, and as he stood there, his hands clasped behind his back, waiting, she fought the urge to run into his arms and kiss him as hard as she could.

Theo looked at him in disbelief.

"That's my name," little Linc looked up at the stranger.

"It is?" Lincoln smiled as he knelt down in front of the boy and looked him in the face. "You look like your mommy."

"I do?" Little Linc brightened up.

"You do, little man. It's very nice to meet you."

"How... How are you here?" Chloe looked as though she might faint as Abi held her up.

"I needed to be here, Chlo. I'm sorry to turn up this way." Lincoln's green eyes bore into Chloe's as rage and excitement battled against the grief that threatened to overcome her.

He stared at her for a moment too long, taking in the black scarf that covered her bald head, and her eyes that seemed to be too large for her gaunt face.

She touched her scarf, suddenly self-conscious.

He looked away, trying to hide the pain in his eyes. He had missed everything. His sister, the woman he had loved. Chloe had gone through her battle alone, this much he knew. He hated himself for what he had done, even though he knew there had been no other choice.

"Where have you been? I mean... why now? Why not when Gina was here?" Chloe cried.

"I c-c-couldn't... Chloe. I shouldn't be here now. Can we just get through this and I'll explain everything? I promise." He moved closer to her, her heart pounding hard in her chest.

Chloe nodded, stepping back from him.

He took a step toward the casket and Chloe and Theo moved away, giving him space.

Chloe held Abi's hand, still trying to believe her eyes.

They watched as Lincoln bent over the casket and whispered to Gina as though she might hear him. When he stood up, his eyes were full of tears and Chloe fought the urge to wipe them away.

He turned and held Chloe's gaze, then his face crumbled in grief.

Even though Chloe was furious with him for staying away, all she could think about was how much she wanted to be in his arms comforting him.

She turned and hid her face from him and wondered if he felt the same way.

 34 ❧

A bi

ABI REMEMBERED LINCOLN AND HOW MUCH CHLOE HAD LOVED HIM.

When he was around, there was nobody else.

Seeing him at the funeral home was shocking to everyone, but especially to Chloe.

He was never her type, but he had the bad boy look going for him with his thick wavy blond hair that looked like it had never seen a comb, and his glittering green eyes. He and Gina resembled one another but while Gina was tiny, Lincoln towered over most people. He had a lean athletic build and wasn't afraid to get into a scuffle anytime the situation called for it.

Chloe had been head over heels for him, but then he had disappeared, and Abi watched Chloe try to move on with her life. She held Chloe's hand tight as her sister kept her eyes on Lincoln, unable to believe he was there.

She had listened to Chloe cry herself to sleep night after night when he disappeared and part of her wanted to punch him in the face for her sister's sake.

As they said their final goodbyes to Gina, the air seemed to be sucked from the room, everyone struggling with their own pain. Lincoln and Leo cried, not understanding that it would be the last time they would see their mom.

Abi took them and Savi out of the room as they closed the casket. She heard the moans of anguish from Theo, Chloe, and Lincoln from the other side of the door.

Within the next fifteen minutes, people began to file into the lobby for the funeral service. To her surprise, the man she had met at the Cathead, David Long was among those filing in.

"David." Abi tried to hide the surprise from her voice. She had thought about calling him several times since their meeting but hadn't made up her mind.

"Abi." His easy smile gave her comfort.

"I didn't realize that you knew Gina and Theo." Abi knew she shouldn't be surprised. Grey's Harbor was small and everyone seemed to be connected in one way or another.

"I work with Theo and coincidentally, my daughter ... the one I was telling you about ... is a nurse. She took care of Mrs. Davidson and the baby at the hospital. We wanted to come and pay our respects. We like both of them very much."

Just then a beautiful girl with dark spiraled curls that framed her face walked in holding hands with Gavin Grey.

"Abi, I'd like you to meet my daughter, Neena, and her boyfriend, Gavin."

Abi stared at the trio, stunned, "Hi..."

"Hi, it's nice to meet you. I actually met Gina several times and was saddened to hear of her passing. How do you know her?" Gavin reached out his hand.

"She was my sister's best friend. I've known her for most of my life." Abi was struck by how down-to-earth he was. She had never actually talked to him even though they were in school together, but they hadn't travelled in the same circles.

Gavin gave her a shy smile and followed Neena to sign the guest book.

"Thank you so much for coming." Abi put her hand out to shake David's hand, and as he took her hand in his, she felt the warmth radiate through her. Seeing him filled her with a strange longing as she pushed it out of her mind to focus on the day. She knew she shouldn't stray too far from Chloe in case she needed her.

"Let me know if you need anything. Our family would be happy to help." David looked at her with kind eyes and Abi smiled gratefully. There was something about him she liked, although she couldn't put her finger on it. She knew there was nothing she could do about it now and hoped there might be a chance later.

People began to pour into the lobby and David, Neena, and Gavin Grey disappeared into the crowd. The Henderson's hurried to find more chairs, and it appeared that all of Grey's Harbor had come to pay their respects. Abi knew that Gina would've been embarrassed by it all since she never liked anyone to make a big deal about her.

Abi wiped away the tears that fell down her cheeks. She hadn't been as close to Gina, but Gina had taught her how to put lipstick on, and when she and Chloe would fight, Gina was the one who helped smooth it over. Abi was the little sister that Gina never had and she would miss her.

Abi watched as Chloe and Lincoln did their best to stay near one another, but avoid each other as well, their chemistry still palpable. She knew that Chloe must be furious with him, but she also remembered that she could never remain angry with Lincoln for long. He was always able to charm her with his kisses and the love he had for her, but this was different. He had clearly been able to return for her and hadn't, and Abi didn't know if Chloe would ever be able to forgive him.

She caught Lincoln stealing glances at her sister, a mixture of sorrow and love in his eyes, and she wondered if Chloe could feel it, too. She wondered what could have possibly kept him away from Gina and Chloe all of those years. How would he possibly ever explain it?

She watched Chloe carefully. She had postponed her treatment for a week, and as hard as she tried to hide it, Abi knew she wasn't doing well.

Chloe sat in the front row, staring silently at the casket, oblivious to the rest of the mourners who filed by paying their respects and giving their condolences to Theo who stood with his arms around Linc and Leo. Lincoln finally settled into a chair two seats over from Chloe, stealing glances that were unreturned. She sat with Savi, like a statue, unwilling to be spoken to or touched.

Abi understood. This is how Chloe had gotten through every hard thing in her life.

Alone.

Hardened.

Untouched.

The only person she had ever allowed in was Gina, and now that she was gone, Abi wondered if Chloe would ever allow anyone else in again.

The service was short and simple, and when it was over, Chloe remained in her seat until everyone had gone. Those who attempted to console her were met with silence or a nod, until it became clear that there would be no consolation. The only person she responded to was Savi, who eventually put her head on her lap as she stroked her long dark hair.

"Chloe, we have to go to the cemetery now. They won't move the casket until you come." Abi touched her arm lightly.

"I c-c-can't..." Chloe spoke as though it hurt her.

"Please, we just have to get in the car."

"No."

Abi stood feeling helpless as Lincoln entered the room and put his hand on her shoulder.

"Let me try."

Abi stepped back as Lincoln approached Chloe like a caged animal. She gestured for Savi to come closer to her as her niece obediently came to her side, sensing something was wrong.

"Chlo... they have to come and take her... so we can go to the cemetery and say our final good-byes. We have to go now, love." Lincoln put his hand on hers and looked her in the eyes.

When Chloe looked at him it was as though she was seeing him for the first time.

"Lincoln!" her voice was surprised.

"It's me, love. We have to go."

"I can't. I can't go. I'm waiting for Gina and if I leave, I'll miss her." Chloe spoke as though she were in a dream.

"She's going with us, love. We have to say our good-byes." Lincoln placed his hand gently on the side of her face, trying to ignore the hollowness in her cheek.

"I can't say good-bye. I don't know how I can live without her." Her voice broke as she said the words, tears welling in her eyes.

"She'll always be here." Lincoln placed his hand on Chloe's heart. "She'll always be with us."

"No!" Chloe stood up suddenly. "I don't want her in there! I want her here, with me. Always! Without her... I'm ..."

"You're perfect." Lincoln finished for her.

"Then why did you leave? Why didn't you come back for me? If I was so perfect, then why did you stay away?" Chloe's eyes were suddenly clear, her voice angry and strong.

"I didn't have a choice, Chlo. Please believe me when I tell you." Lincoln looked at her, desperate to explain. "I couldn't come home, but I looked after you as best as I could. I tried. I just couldn't be here."

"Then how are you here now? Why are you able to be here now?"

Abi felt a knot in the pit of her stomach. Something told her the answer wouldn't be good.

"Please, Chloe. Can we put my sister to rest, and then I promise, I'll tell you everything? Please?" Lincoln cautiously put his hand on Chloe's shoulder.

Chloe paused, and for a moment, Abi thought she was going to continue fighting, but she relented.

"Yes."

As they turned and walked out of the funeral home, Lincoln caught Abi's eye and Abi could see the one thing that Chloe could not. It was the one thing Chloe could never seem to see in anyone.

Even herself.

Fear.

35

C hloe

CHLOE SAT AT THE GRAVESITE AND STARED AT THE CASKET.

She held Savi on her lap and sat as still as she could. She was afraid to breathe or even move. She thought that if she did, she might shatter into a million broken pieces and she didn't want to do that in front of Savi.

Or even Lincoln for that matter.

She knew how she must look to him anyway.

She could see the shock in his eyes at how emaciated and sickly she looked. He would be surprised to know that she looked better than she had in months. She had even managed to put on a few pounds with this treatment.

She knew that he must pity her and she hated it. She didn't want anything from him, especially not pity. What she did want was an explanation for why he never came back for her or Gina, and after that she never wanted anything from him ever again.

After the brief service, she gave Theo and the boys time alone at the casket, and when they finally left, she took her place. As though reading her mind, Abi gently took Savi's hand and lead her toward the car where they would wait, as long as it took. Chloe gave her a grateful look. She and Abi had grown close since her mother had insisted on Abi moving in to take care of her.

At first Chloe fought against the obvious manipulation to bring her and her sister closer together, but in the end she was grateful. She had forgotten how much she had loved having Abi near, pushing it out of her mind for years to block the hurt of her being gone.

Chloe tried to ignore Lincoln as he lingered behind as well, and she knew she needed to give him time, but she resented it and him.

She stared at the casket still unable to believe that Gina was inside.

"Why? Why would you leave me? How can I ever do this without you?" she whispered in anguish. For a brief second, she let her heart go, and as she did, it broke apart, thrusting her to the ground as she cried like a wounded animal.

Lincoln rushed over to her.

"Love!"

She allowed herself to be wrapped in his arms.

She emptied herself of tears as he held her as tightly as he could without hurting her. He thought that if he held her tight enough it might help her heal, and then she might forgive him. As she sobbed in his arms, he cried as well, all of the years of loneliness and longing for Gina and Chloe welling up inside of him in deep waves.

Holding Chloe made him feel less alone and he never wanted to let her go. He held her for a long time, and when she was finally empty she looked up at him, her cheeks stained with tears.

"Why, Lincoln? Why did you leave us? Why didn't you come back?"

It was the moment he knew he would have to answer to, the one he had dreaded for years. Everything he had done to keep them safe would never be enough because they would never understand, and now he would never get the chance to explain it to Gina.

Theo, in his grief, had shown no interest in his presence or his absence, although he was hoping he could talk to him, too. Lincoln knew the window was closing, but he wasn't going to force himself on a man who had just lost his wife.

Chloe was the one he was terrified of.

If she didn't understand, he didn't know what he would do.

"I couldn't, love. When I left, I wasn't given a choice. Momma traded me to feed her habit, just like she did with Gina. The man she traded me to was the top guy for a big-time dealer who made me stay and work for him, doing things I never imagined I would ever have to do. I wasn't given a choice, Chlo. He was a ... bad ... awful man, and if I didn't do what he wanted me to there would be consequences, for all of you. I had to do everything he wanted to keep you safe."

Chloe couldn't believe her ears. Grey's Harbor was a safe, sleepy town. How could all of this go on in front of everyone?

"I've been everywhere, Chlo. He didn't operate just in the harbor. This was just a tiny blip on his radar, nothing really." Lincoln went on as if reading her mind, and Chloe suddenly felt unsafe and exposed.

"How .... Did you know about Gina? How did she know she was gone?"

Lincoln hesitated.

"I've kept tabs on all of you. I knew about your cancer and about Gina. I have contacts here that keep me informed... I've moved up in the organization ... over the years. Like I said earlier, I wasn't given a choice."

Chloe pulled away from him.

"What does that mean? That you're... "

"It means that I can't stay here ... with you. It means that every second I spend here puts you in danger, but I had to say good-bye to my sister. I had to, and I had to see you one more time. I've never been able to forget you, Chloe. There's never been anyone else who compares to you." Lincoln's green eyes bore into Chloe's, and as the rest of the world fell away, she wanted to beg him to stay.

"You had a choice! You could've come back anytime." Chloe seethed in anger. "All of those years you were away, we thought you were dead. We thought you had been killed, but instead, you've been living this ... life ..."

"No. I couldn't. You don't understand and I don't want you to. I shouldn't be here now. It was selfish of me and I am putting you in danger just by being here with you. I can't stay, Chloe. As much as I want to, as much as I've always loved you and not been able to get you out of my heart, I can't stay. I am living the sins of my parents, and there is nothing I can do to change that." Lincoln took her hand and kissed her palm.

Chloe let out a wounded cry and allowed him to hold her as she tried to wrap her thoughts around everything he had told her. Even as kids, somehow she had always known they would never get to be together forever, but she had always hoped.

"When?"

"I'm leaving from the cemetery. If I could hold you in my arms and forget the world around us, I would do it without a second's thought. But you have your daughter, Abi and her kids, and I can't stay. I can't risk something happening to you. If certain people knew where I was and who I was with... that's why I have to leave now."

"When I saw you, I wanted to punish you, but then I wanted you to stay with me forever. I don't know that I will ever allow myself to love anyone like I loved you." Chloe pulled his body as close to hers as she could. "I don't know if I can let you go."

"You have to, love." He fought the urge to moan in agony as he kissed her lips. He had never wanted to leave her, and for a second, he thought he should ask her to go with him, but he pushed it far from his mind. He could never take her and her daughter out of the safety of Grey's Harbor. There was no place for them in his world, and Chloe deserved the chance to be safe *and* have love, neither of which he could give her at the same time, and he knew she deserved better.

"Why did you come back if you're just going to go away? Don't you know that I've never stopped loving you?"

"It was selfish, and I'm sorry. I just had to... say goodbye to Gina. I was there when she got married, but she never saw me. I've been trying to look out for both of you as much as possible... but my life is dangerous in ways that you could never imagine, and as much as it kills me, I could never take you with me. I'm so sorry, love." Lincoln held her gaze for longer than he wanted.

"Am I ever going to see you again?"

"I don't know but I'll keep checking on you. Just promise me that you won't wait for me. I won't be back to stay... ever."

She nodded as she looked up at him. She knew she could never put Savi's life in danger, and as much as it broke her heart to lose him again, there was no other choice.

He walked her to the car where Savi sat, her nose pressed against the window staring out at them.

As he helped her in the car, Chloe could feel every piece of herself begin to fall apart. Any strength she had left was gone as she sat down in a crumbled heap.

"I'll always love you, Chloe," Lincoln said, giving her one final kiss.

As Abi pulled the car away, Chloe watched Lincoln out of the window, and as he grew smaller, she wished he had never returned.

Losing him once was heartbreaking, but she didn't know if she would ever be able to recover after losing him twice.

❧ 36 ❧

ONE YEAR LATER

Neena

Neena sat in a booth at the Cathead across from Vanessa.

Vanessa looked better than she had for as long as Neena could remember, and she was happy for Jaden's sake. Jaden had missed his mother, and now that she was clean, and had been for over five months, the court had been more lenient on her visitation.

Vanessa resembled more of the mother that Neena had always hoped she would be, and Neena was happy to see her mom healthy.

"I'm having chicken fingers, Nee," Jaden said, smiling at his sister.

"The Cathead has good chicken fingers, Jay." Neena smiled back, marveling at how much she had been smiling in the past year.

When Vanessa had first texted her again after stealing her book money, she responded but refused to meet her right away. After a month she finally agreed, but Gavin had insisted on going along.

"I'd like to meet your momma if you are all right with that, baby." Gavin was protective but didn't smother her, and Neena loved that about him. He didn't see her as the broken little girl of a drug addict, and neither did his family. "You've taken care of your daddy, your brother, and gone to school and graduated in the top of your class."

Gavin was good to her. Far better than she ever thought she deserved or would ever have. She had watched her father suffer for love her entire life and never imagined someone could ever love her. Neena still woke up most days and had to pinch herself that Gavin Grey loved her.

"I got a job, Neena." Vanessa's voice was quiet, but proud. She looked almost shy as she avoided Neena's eyes.

"You did, Momma? Where?" Neena was surprised. She had never known Vanessa to work. As she took her in, she almost seemed like a completely different person than she had grown up to know. Her long hair was braided artfully, her beautiful caramel colored skin almost glowing. She had put on a few pounds and no longer had the gaunt look of someone whose diet consisted of street drugs and alcohol.

When she had come back into Neena's life, Neena demanded she get help if she ever wanted to see Jaden or her ever again. Gavin had insisted on paying for her to go to an intensive wellness facility an hour outside of Grey's Harbor for a month, and Vanessa had reluctantly agreed. She had nowhere else to go and nobody else to turn to.

Rehabilitation had never worked for her before, she had insisted, but this time was different. She knew she would die if she didn't allow someone to help her, and Gavin had chosen this facility with Emerson's help. It was reputable and effective, and Vanessa allowed them to dig into the years of sexual abuse she had suffered as a young girl, which had finally helped heal her spirit as well as her body.

When she came out, Neena was amazed that she seemed like a different person altogether. It was a gift she could never repay Gavin for as long as she lived.

"At the library," Vanessa smiled. "You know how much I love books. I'll be able to be around them all day, every day."

Just then Emerson fell into the booth next to her, flustered. She clumsily plopped a stack of magazines and a large portfolio on the table.

"I'm so sorry that I'm late," she hugged Vanessa hurriedly and kissed Jaden on top of his head. "What did I hear you say about the library?"

"Momma got a job at the library," Neena smiled proudly.

"Oh, that's wonderful!" Emerson hugged Vanessa again. Vanessa smiled shyly. She wasn't used to being the center of attention and was still overwhelmed by the Grey's. She never expected them to take to her, but they treated her like a person and not like an ex-addict like most people in town did.

Vanessa had spent the better part o her life hiding in the shadows, living in the dark, and being around people like Emerson and Lillian who treated her like she was someone as important as they were made her feel strange. In the best possible way.

"Thank you." Vanessa hugged her back.

"Okay, let's get down to business." Emerson set her blue eyes evenly on Neena's. "We have a wedding we need to plan."

Neena glowed.

"Yes, we do." Neena thought about Gavin and how deeply she had fallen in love with him.

He was perfect in every way.

He was everything she'd always wanted but never thought she deserved even though he protested any time she said anything.

"It's me who doesn't deserve you," Gavin repeated, kissing the tip of her nose. "Someone like you who is as strong, beautiful, and smart and yet chooses me.... I'm the lucky one!"

When he asked her to marry him last month, with his great-grandmother's ring, she was flabbergasted. He had done it during her birthday, in front of all of their family and friends at the Grey House. Emerson had insisted on throwing her a big party in her beautiful home even though Neena had protested.

Like Vanessa, she wasn't used to being the center of attention, but Emerson promised to keep it casual and light, and she had. She had even convinced Neena's daddy, David, and his girlfriend, Abi to help them celebrate. Abi had been timid about joining the family because of their age difference, but Neena liked her with David. It had been too long since David had been loved by anyone.

His marriage to Vanessa had nearly ruined him but with Abi, he had a newfound confidence that Neena had never seen him have before. She was surprised that he looked younger than she'd ever remembered him looking, his grief and worry always stressing him so much.

"What do you want to do for your wedding?" Emerson asked, after the waitress had taken everyone's order.

"We just want something simple," Neena said hopefully.

"Yes..." Emerson chewed on her pen thoughtfully. "But... he's a Grey, and you will be, too. We don't do anything simply, especially not weddings. Unfortunately, sweet girl, this wedding is going to be one of the biggest affairs on the Harbor."

Neena frowned. "How big are we talking?"

"Huge!" Emerson gushed. "But you're going to have so much fun! I promise. It'll be completely all about you, and you're going to love it. Will you give me permission to help plan this for you?"

From the moment Neena met Emerson, she had loved her and knew that she would never do something that Neena would hate. She trusted her as she nodded.

"Excellent!" Emerson was grinning from ear to ear. She thought about her wedding six months ago to Evan and how perfect it had been. She loved weddings and new beginnings. Her heart was full and was about to get even fuller. "We can get this together pretty quickly if that's okay with you."

"Yes," Neena said, putting her hand on her belly. "I'd like to get it done as soon as possible, before these two make me any fatter."

Emerson nodded.

"We'll get this bash planned for the next month! Trust me, I'm an expert at these things," Emerson winked at the woman carrying her grandchildren.

Neena rubbed her stomach, enjoying the slight roundness of it. Having twins was terrifying, but Gavin was thrilled, and she was caught up in the excitement of it all. He didn't like to do anything in half measures, and she was finding that life with him had become a wonderful and exciting adventure.

She thought about the past twelve months and grinned at Vanessa.

It had been one hell of a year.

❧ 37 ❧

C hloe

"KIDS, LET'S GET READY FOR SCHOOL." CHLOE GULPED DOWN THE last bit of her coffee and clapped her hands.

Six little feet came running and it sounded like a herd of elephants running down the hall.

"What are we eating?" The boys were always hungry and Chloe laughed.

"We're eating eggs and bacon." Chloe smiled as she poured them juice.

"Do we have strawberries, Mommy?" Savi asked sweetly.

"Yes, we have strawberries, honey. They're on the table," Chloe put some on her plate. She kissed Savi on the top of her head, affectionately. Boys and girls were so different, and there were times when the boys made Chloe's head pound. She wasn't used to so much noise but was trying hard to get accustomed to it.

So much had changed in the past year and she was still working her way around it all. The last treatment had been successful, and she had been so thrilled to ring the final bell when it was over. She was even more thrilled when the oncologist told her that the last round of treatment had worked and that her tumor was gone. Her energy level was getting better and she was happy to finally be moving forward with her busy life.

The grief she had been working through in the last year required help, and while she was tempted to drink it away, she knew that wine wasn't going to help. Nothing was going to help except continuing to go through the therapy she had started when she was first diagnosed with cancer.

Therapy and Theo.

That was what was getting her through and keeping her breathing day after day.

At first, they had leaned on one another, their grief understood only by the other.

Abi did everything she could to be there for her, but she was finally filing for divorce and had started dating David, which came with it an entirely different set of complications. Her parents had been less than thrilled that Abi was dating a man so much older than she was, which had thankfully taken the focus off of Chloe, her cancer, and her friendship with Theo.

There were many long nights when Chloe would fall asleep and wake up with her phone in her hand and a tear stained face. Theo had been on the other end of the line and had woken up the same. Their weekly trips to the cemetery began to end in coffee, and then wine, and then finally dinners that lasted late into the night, neither of them wanting to admit that their bond was more than just shared grief.

Seeing Lincoln at Gina's funeral was surprisingly healing for Chloe. While she had initially been devastated, she was finally able to move on. Her divorce from Brent had been surprisingly painless. He hadn't wanted anything and was willing to give her everything. He had finally begun to see Savi on a regular basis, and Chloe's tangled heart began to unravel and find peace.

While she had always thought that Theo was handsome, she had never been attracted to him when Gina was alive. Their bond had been too tight and she could never have imagined betraying her.

"I always knew you were beautiful, Chloe, but honestly, I never looked at any other woman except for Gina," Theo had admitted, bashfully.

When they were out, people were taken by surprise at their collective attractiveness, but neither ever seemed to notice. The only thing they were able to see was one another, and Chloe realized that she had never known what it meant to love someone until Theo.

A year later, and they had decided to combine their families. Chloe often worried that it was too soon as she stared at the photos of Gina, Theo, and the boys that remained up around Gina's house, the home they now shared together. Theo had offered to take them down or move them, but Chloe had refused.

She had to believe that Gina would be happy that they were together because the two people that she had loved the most had found comfort and a safe harbor in one another. Most days, Chloe was able to push the guilt away, but other days she still struggled.

"Breakfast is good, Chloe!" Lincoln and Leo loved Chloe's cooking. They gulped down the rest of their juice and tore down the hall to get their bags together for school.

"Boys," Savi shook her head and she and Chloe laughed.

Chloe was impressed with how well she had adjusted to their new family. Savi adored Frannie, and Chloe was happy that Frannie was surrounded by so much love, even if her mother wasn't there. She resembled Gina more and more every day, and Chloe found that loving her was so easy.

Theo came into the kitchen, buttoning his cuffs.

"Good morning, darling." Theo kissed Chloe on the cheek. "You look beautiful today."

Chloe smiled. She had learned to stop protesting when Theo complimented her. She knew that her hair was slightly mussed and that without makeup on, she felt less attractive but none of that mattered. Theo only saw the good in her, just as he had with Gina, and she adored that about him. He had taught her to do the same and she no longer saw the gaps and fissures in others that she used to, including herself.

Limiting her time with Anita helped, but with four children, including a new baby, she didn't have as much time as she used to. She had given up her stressful job to stay home with the kids, something she never imagined she would do, but she loved it.

Especially her time with Frannie, and for the first time in her life, she allowed herself to be happy.

The first time Theo kissed her, Chloe looked into his deep brown eyes and fell into them. She finally understood what it meant to completely love another individual who wasn't your child, and she realized how much she had missed over the years. While her love for Lincoln was passionate and exciting, it couldn't compare to what she was falling into with Theo.

"I think Gina would be happy that I love you," Theo said when they decided to combine their families. "If there was anyone in the universe she would want me to love, it would definitely be you."

As Chloe watched Frannie grow, her beautiful bright eyes alert and intelligent, she made sure to tell her about Gina every day. "I'm your momma, but your Momma Gina loved you so much, and you are as beautiful as she is."

"Momma G," Frannie said, giggling. She loved when Chloe told her about Momma G.

As the kids ran out for the bus, they took turns giving Chloe and Frannie kisses.

"Have a good day, little loves," Chloe called out as they waved behind them.

She looked down at Frannie who stood with her nose pressed against the door, watching her brothers and sister run and leave her behind.

"I go..." she pointed as she looked up at Chloe.

"Not yet, baby girl." Chloe scooped her up and kissed her cheeks until she giggled, trying to remember when her life had ever been so perfect. "Not yet."

38

A bi

TODD HAD FINALLY SIGNED THE DIVORCE PAPERS, AND ABI WAS
ecstatic. It had taken quite some time to track him down. He had
already moved on from Cat, leaving her with a new baby, but that was
none of Abi's concern.

She had just wanted to be free of him.

Since she was suing him for child support, she knew she would
never see him again which was sad for Lexi and Dom who were getting
older and understanding more about choices.

When she finally received word from her lawyer that the divorce
was final, she was thrilled.

"I just feel... so free," she took a long drink of her beer as she sat on
a bar stool at the Mizzen Mast, her legs in between David's long ones
that were resting on the bottom of her stool.

"Cheers to being free." David held up his mug and toasted her,
their glasses clinking together.

After their first meeting at the Cathead Diner when he had given her his card, then seeing her at the funeral for Gina Davidson, he hadn't been able to stop thinking about her. Something about her had seeped into the edges of his mind and he found himself wanting to talk to her every day. He couldn't explain it since they hadn't spent much time together, but the attraction was there, and it wasn't going away.

When she called him a couple of weeks after the funeral and asked if he was handy because their garbage disposal was jammed, he knew it was excuse, and his heart jumped at the thought of it. As they spent more time together, he began to question what she would see in him.

He had worked hard for Jaden, to stay fit and healthy. He didn't want his son to have a daddy that couldn't keep up with him. But he was boring and broken, and for the life of him he couldn't imagine what a beautiful young woman would ever see in him, but she liked him.

It was clear.

When she asked if they could spend some time together, he nearly told her 'no' and as the last minute agreed. He had been alone too long, but he wasn't sure if being alone was going to be harder than being with someone else, especially someone who might realize in a few months that he wasn't worth it.

He looked around to see if anyone was watching them, a habit he couldn't seem to break. With their thirteen-year age difference, he still felt awkward about being in public with her.

"Please stop doing that," Abi scolded him.

"I know... I just ..." he tried to hide his embarrassment. "I just don't want people to think that I'm a dirty old guy."

"But you are." Abi looked at him with a straight face, then burst out laughing, gently taking his face in her hands. "David, you are the kindest, gentlest, most amazing man I've ever met and you deserve to be happy. We deserve to be happy, and you aren't doing anything wrong."

David nodded as he kissed her on the lips to show her that he understood.

He was happy.

Abi made him happier than he had been for as long as he could remember, and the only person's approval he had needed the most was

Neena's. Much to his surprise, she was thrilled for him and didn't care at all about Abi's age.

"Daddy, I just want you to be happy and to move on from Momma. After all of these years, you deserve to be happy," Neena told him the day he told her about Abi. She pointed to his wedding ring that he had refused to take off long after Vanessa had left him. "Momma left you a long time ago, and she treated you horribly, and even though she's sorry now, you deserve someone who is going to love you."

David was appreciative of Neena's blessing but held his breath every time Neena and Abi were in the same room. Abi wasn't going to be a mother figure to her, but he hoped they could at least be friends. He was happy to see that they were off to a good start, both women genuinely interested in the other's well being, but he remained uncertain of Abi, waiting for her to break his heart.

He fought the urge to look around the bar, to see if anyone was looking at them.

"Don't do it, buddy," Abi warned him.

He looked at her and concentrated on her face. He could never seem to take his eyes off of her when she was in the room. Her big blue eyes pulled him in as he pushed a stray curl behind her ear. Her smile made him forget everything and everyone around him as he leaned in and kissed her once more.

"Get a room," Izzy, the owner of the Mizzen Mast quipped.

Izzy knew everyone in town and had a special fondness for the brutally broken. She'd known for years about David and had watched Neena grow up without her momma. She and Maeve often compared notes about their mutual guests, especially the ones they felt the worst for and were the most hurt.

Vanessa's earliest subterfuge had been brutal and public, with much of the town witnessing the highs and lows that came with her addiction. Izzy sympathized with Vanessa, struggling for years with her own demons, even though she didn't excuse what Vanessa had done to her family. She was happy to hear that Vanessa had done well coming out of rehab and even happier still that David had finally seemed to move on.

"I hear that Neena and Gavin are engaged." Izzy gave David a knowing smile.

"Yes! We're very excited."

"And..." Izzy prodded.

"And... they're having twins."

Izzy's face lit up and David reached out and hugged her. Izzy had the reputation of being a hard ass, but David had seen the softness in her many times.

"It's going to be a great year," David ordered another beer for him and Abi.

"Yes, it is," Abi reached up and kissed him again.

"Now that Chloe has moved in with Theo and she is doing much better, what are you going to do when she sells the house?" David asked cautiously.

"I've already been looking at a place for the kids and I." Abi thought about how much she was going to miss living with Chloe. They had become so close over the past year; it was hard to believe there had ever been a wedge between them. "I'm also looking for a job."

"W-w-would you consider moving in with Jaden and me?" David had been thinking about asking her for a while but had been afraid.

Abi looked at him, her eyes wide.

"I don't know, David. That seems so... it's so nice of you... but it's just too..."

"I understand," David put up a hand to stop her. "It was just a suggestion. I know it's early."

"Yes, I ... I care about you a lot, but I don't know that Dom and Lexi are ready for such a big change. As much as I hate to say it, I might move back in with my parents for a little while to save some money and figure out what I'm going to do next."

Abi would've never considered moving back in with Anita and Anthony, but taking care of Chloe had given her a voice that she'd never had before where her parents were concerned.

"I'm an adult, Momma, and I'm old enough to make decisions for myself and my children. I don't care if you don't like it, and if you don't start showing me some respect, our relationship is going to be finished.

I can't do this any longer." Abi had finally exploded, and Anita had been dramatically offended, but had been on her best behavior since.

"Maybe one day, when you're ready, we can talk about it again?" David smiled.

"Yes, we can," Abi took his hand in hers.

She had never met anyone who was so perfect for her, who made her feel like she was perfect, and she knew there would be a day when David Long would be her husband.

❧ 39 ❧

eena

EMERSON HAD FULFILLED HER PROMISE AND PLANNED THE PERFECT wedding. It had only taken her a month to plan, and it looked like the entire harbor had come to attend the wedding of Gavin Grey and Neena Long.

As Neena looked at herself in the mirror she was in awe of the reflection looking back at her. She had never in all of her wildest dreams imagined that she could ever look so beautiful. Her long dress, accented with beads and lace, disguised her bump beautifully. Her beautiful curls had been tamed and her beaded headdress flowed elegantly down her back.

She was glowing.

The knock on the door took her out of her reverie.

As Vanessa entered the room, Neena was surprised to see that there were few traces of the addict left. She looked graceful in her sea foam green mother-of-the-bride dress, her nails and hair expertly done for the occasion. Tears pricked Neena's eyes at the sight of her.

"You look beautiful," she breathed.

Vanessa laughed, a shy embarrassed laugh. "I look beautiful? Oh, my sweet doll, you look beautiful. Beyond anything I have ever seen."

Neena willed herself not to cry.

"I just ... wanted to stop by ... and say something to you, if that's okay." Vanessa took a step toward Neena and then stopped.

Neena nodded.

"I... have been the worst mother a human being can be."

"Momma..." Neena protested.

"No, I need to say this to you." Vanessa's voice was firm as Neena nodded. "I... I've had terrible things happen to me in my childhood, but I made the choice to cope with them the wrong way. I didn't have a momma to teach me and help me, but then neither did you. You didn't have a momma either, and I'm so sorry about that."

Vanessa's voice caught.

"You were... the perfect child. You were ... and are ... the perfect daughter. I know you spent your entire life trying to figure out what you could do to make me better, or make me stay but I want you to know that you were always... perfect."

Neena rushed into Vanessa's arms and they held one another for a long moment, tears flowing freely.

"I'm so sorry, my sweet doll. I'm so sorry for the awful mother I've been to you."

"You can change that now," Neena said stepping back and placing her hand on Vanessa's cheek. "You can be there for me now and be that perfect mother now because we have a second chance."

Vanessa nodded.

"You would be willing to give that to me after everything I've done?"

"Yes." Neena kissed her on the cheek. "Yes. I would because Grey's Harbor is a wonderful place for second chances. Look at us. We can do this, together."

Vanessa nodded, wiping her tears.

"I can do that. I can be a better mother. I will be a better mother to you... and Jaden. Both of you deserve it."

There was a knock on the door and David popped his head into the room, suddenly alarmed as he saw Vanessa and Neena with mascara and make up running down their faces.

"Its okay Daddy, come in."

He entered the room cautiously.

"I'm sorry, David. I ... want to be better ... for all of you. I know how much I've hurt you, but I want a chance to do what's right. Please forgive me."

David nodded as he took Vanessa in his arms, his body towering over her. "I forgive you Vanessa."

The door flew open as Emerson came in, followed by Joy, who owned Joyful Cuts. She had done their hair and make up and entered the room with a large black bag in her hand.

"What in the hell?" Joy said as she looked at Vanessa, then Neena, then back to Vanessa. "What did you do to my work? Look at your faces? Good God!"

Emerson laughed gently. "You can fix them, right?"

Joy shot her a dirty look. "Of course I can."

Neena looked at Emerson questioningly.

"I saw your Momma headed this way and I assumed you all would need some help." Emerson shrugged her shoulders and winked at Neena. "This isn't my first rodeo, kiddo."

As both women sat and let Joy repair the damage their tears had done, Emerson ushered everyone out of the room.

David walked to the back of the church, blowing a kiss to Abi on his way.

Neena closed her eyes and sighed.

Emerson left the room with strict orders to Joy to make sure she escorted them both to the back of the church to get ready for the processional.

"No shortcuts, anywhere," she demanded.

Joy agreed, already busy repairing Vanessa's makeup and muttering to herself.

As Emerson looked out into the church, she was pleased at the turnout. It looked like most of Grey's Harbor had come for Gavin's wedding. She looked up toward the sky and smiled.

"You would be proud of our boy, Sawyer," she whispered. "He's marrying the perfect girl and you would be so happy."

A tear slipped down her cheek.

She saw Theo and Chloe in the crowd, her heart falling for a minute as she thought about how lovely Gina had been. She knew how close Gina and Chloe had been and thought that if anything could help the two of them heal, it would be their collective love for Gina and each other. Her heart burst with happiness as she saw Maeve and Tank, Jaxx and Maddy, Bridger and Hope, Jennifer and Ryker, and so many other residents of Grey's Harbor that made up the fabric of the town. She had made sure that everyone was invited to celebrate her beautiful son and daughter-in-law on their big day.

She winked at Lillian who stood waiting to be escorted to the front by Garrett. He had finally brought his girlfriend home to meet them and she felt her heart bursting with happiness and pride. As the music began, she took her place in the back of the church and looped her arm through Ethan's. He looked down and smiled at her, appreciating how beautiful she looked.

As the wedding began, Emerson realized how happy she was to live in such a beautiful town as Grey's Harbor.

There was no place in the world she could ever imagine living.

It wasn't without pain and suffering, but it was beautiful and hopeful.

It was as perfect a place on earth that she would ever want to be.

The End

AFTERWORD

Thank you so much for reading Perfect Seas, A Grey's Harbor Story!

Please help others to find my book by leaving an honest review on Goodreads or Amazon.

Reviews don't have to be long or detailed. They can be one or two lines that simply state how you felt about the book! It helps readers want to take a chance on a new-to-them author and we appreciate it so very much!

If you'd like to keep up with me, please join my email list and you'll receive a free eCopy of Leaving Eva, the first book in the Eva Series, as well as updates and news about my author journey.

Thank you so much for reading!

X,

Jennifer

ACKNOWLEDGMENTS

As I wrote this story in Grey's Harbor, I began to wish once again that this was a real place.

When Lark Griffing, JC Wing, and I began to create this universe we didn't realize how much we would fall in love with it. As we continue our journey creating this universe, we are inspired and excited to see Grey's Harbor grow and evolve and the love our readers have for it.

When you find synergy with two amazing artists like I have with Lark and JC, there's magic. I am so fortunate to have found that with these two women who inspire, encourage, challenge, and love me every day.

Kate Conway, of Wicked Whale Publishing is a wonderfully talented designer and I love the work she did on the cover. It's like she read my mind and knew exactly what this story needed.

As always, I'm so thankful for my amazing family and wonderful readers. I'm so fortunate that I get to write and share the stories in my head and heart, and I hope you continue to visit us in Grey's Harbor.

ABOUT THE AUTHOR

Jennifer Sivec writes beautifully broken stories with heart.

She is attracted to and writes stories with characters that are complicated, flawed and completely imperfect. Her books are often a reflection of life, encompassing difficult subjects such as cancer, addiction, abandonment, and abuse. She writes with a raw, complex, yet hopeful approach often weaving tragic stories with honesty and grace, creating unforgettable characters.

Jennifer has been writing since she was in the fourth grade but didn't publish her first novel until 2014, and has been writing non- stop since. Her passion for reading and sharing stories gives her perspective and peace of mind.

She lives in Ohio with her husband, two boys, herd of dogs who create balance and levity for her. She loves her crazy life and wonderful readers, and is grateful for all of it, every day.

ALSO BY JENNIFER SIVEC